The Range

Elizabeth Bromke

To receive special offers, exclusive content, and other sweet romances, sign up for my newsletter at elizabethbromke.com[1]

Become an exclusive Bookworm. Join me on Facebook[2]!

Never miss a deal. Follow me on BookBub[3]!

This book is a work of fiction. Names, characters, places, and events are products of the author's imagination. Any resemblance to locations, events, or people (living or dead) is purely coincidental.
Copyright © 2019 Sarah Bromke
All rights reserved.
Cover design by German Creative
Edited by Krissy Moran
The reproduction or distribution of this book without permission is a theft. If you would like to share this book or any part thereof (reviews excepted), please contact us through our website: elizabethbromke.com
THE RANGER'S MOUNTAIN BRIDE

---

1. https://www.elizabethbromke.com/

2. https://www.facebook.com/groups/bromkesbookworms/

3. https://www.bookbub.com/authors/elizabeth-bromke

Cover design by GermanCreative.
First Edition- October 2019
Published by:
Elizabeth Bromke
White Mountains, Arizona

In Loving Memory of Aunt Margot

Prologue

Eight months earlier...

Air conditioning blasted the smell of freshly baked breads as Keegan Flanagan strode through the automatic doors of Big Ed's Country Market.

Maplewood was a tourist town, and weekends meant crowds of flatlanders—as locals called them. Keegan didn't much mind the influx... until he went grocery shopping.

It took some deft weaving through a growing throng of customers as he grabbed a basket and began to fill it with essentials. Bread, fruits, veggies, a few protein bars, and a couple of frozen entrees took him to the far side of the store.

Once he moved to the dairy section, a barricade of college-aged kids blocked his path. Two girls led the pack. Keegan stepped up against the refrigerated doors and waved his hand like a gentleman to let them pass.

As they neared, the girls in front trained their eyes on him. The tallest even pointed.

"Well hello, Mountain Man," she whispered loudly to her friend, keeping her eyes on Keegan. They fell into wild giggles. Keegan smirked before averting his gaze beyond them to a familiar face. A beautiful face.

Bo Delaney.

"It's like the mountain is a zoo, and we're the animals," she said once the tourists moved on to another aisle.

Keegan's eyes passed over Bo, taking in her dark hair, piercing eyes, and pale skin. Dressed in worn jeans and a plain white T-shirt, it was like she had stepped out of high school and into adulthood without a hitch. She was grown up and gorgeous.

Keegan swallowed hard. He hadn't seen Bo in years. He wondered if she was still into jerks like she had been at Maplewood High before she'd bolted the mountain for greener pastures.

He laughed and nodded his head in agreement. "Back for vacation, *Roberta*?"

"Don't call me that, Keegan." She glared before allowing a smile to spread across her lips. "Not a visit this time." She glanced over her shoulder as another throng of people squeezed by. The two moved closer to the refrigerated case. And each other.

"What does that mean?"

"I'm living here again. Got a job with the paper. Reporter gig. Right now, just fluff pieces, but we're hoping to broaden my section. Got any juicy gossip for me?" She teased as she drew a finger to her mouth and nibbled on the nail.

High school memories flashed through his head. Bo peeking out from the far side of their friend group while they sat five across in a darkened movie theater. Bo throwing a curious glance to Keegan in Spanish class.

Bo.

Bo.

Bo.

She had been too cool back then. Befriending boys over girls and preferring Writer's Guild to cheerleading. A cool, brainy beauty.

His forever crush.

Keegan was aloof in high school. But he saw Bo. Always had. Still did, sometimes, when his Aunt Marg asked if he was dating. Or when his parents wondered why he was turning up to Christmas without a special someone—*again*.

He played along, winking and lowering his voice. "Word has it they may delay the Fourth of July fireworks display by half an hour. But you didn't hear that from me."

She let out a hearty laugh, her face softening and body relaxing. Keegan moved his eyes back to hers. "Well, Bo, in all seriousness, welcome back to the mountain. I, for one, am glad you're here."

Chapter 1

Flames lapped at the iron grate, the logs beneath them popping loudly. Bo tore her eyes away from the mesmerizing fire and stared after Keegan, who carried their dishes from the table to the sink.

They'd dated ever since reconnecting the summer before. Casually, at first. Then things began to change, somehow. Still, it wasn't quite serious.

What Keegan and Bo had together fell somewhere in between—that awkward place in which dating adults eventually find themselves: afraid to use silly labels like boyfriend and girlfriend (they were in their thirties, for goodness' sake) but afraid to ask each other what was next.

Well, Bo came to realize what she wanted next in life. The only problem? She'd never said as much. In fact, at one point in their relationship, she distinctly recalled telling Keegan that she *did not* want to get married. Ever.

Stupid, stupid, stupid.

Insecure, too.

But she'd gotten over the hump of pretending she was above such conventions as marriage. Bo wanted a label.

But she could not be the one to say so. Anyway, she had equally important things to worry about, like the future of her career, namely.

THE RANGER'S MOUNTAIN BRIDE

She swallowed hard as Keegan took care to fill the apron-style tub with hot, soapy water before dunking and scrubbing their plates and silverware.

Muscles rippled beneath his thin white t-shirt, and Bo felt her heart dip to the top of her stomach and bounce back up to her throat. Again, she swallowed and looked back to the fire.

At last, Keegan shelved each plate, fork, and knife in a wooden drying rack.

Bo held back from offering to help. She needed to reserve her energy. Because Bo was about to break his heart. And her own.

There was no stopping the stubborn Roberta Delaney.

"Keegan," she began, as he returned to the table, an empty wineglass in each of his work-worn hands.

"Bo?" he answered, his voice even, his smile fading only just.

Their dinner had been nice. Or as nice as possible. Keegan was no chef, but he could grill a mean burger and whipped together mashed potatoes well enough.

He set the glasses down and, instead of turning for the bottle he'd opened to let breathe, he cocked his hands on his hips, involuntarily flexing his abdomen. Bo closed her eyes, briefly. When she opened them again, Keegan's dark brows lifted into high arches. No smile, now. He was waiting.

"I'm moving."

"In with me? I thought we talked about that. No playing house, right? I mean, Bo, that is a... tantalizing idea, but we made a deal. You stay at Mary's. I stay here." A mischievous grin curled up his cheeks, but it fell as he met Bo's hard gaze.

"No. I'm moving back to Tucson."

Keegan drew a hand to his forehead and scratched it like a dumb cartoon character. Keegan Flanagan was decidedly *not* a dumb cartoon character. He was smart as a whip and handsome as the devil. But moments like this—when Keegan's rough-and-tumble exterior gave way to boyish charm—only added to her heartache over the matter.

"Why would you move back *there*? I thought we already talked about this..."

No. They had not *talked about this*. "No, we didn't."

"Well, you said you liked your job at the paper."

That much was true. Bo enjoyed working for the *Mountain Times*. She did not love it, however. And Bo, if nothing else, was a career woman at heart. She had to *love* her job. It was the only constant in her life. Besides, Keegan was dragging his heels to propose. Maybe he didn't even want marriage. Did Bo? Who knew? But she *did* want the option.

"I think I can do better," she answered, honestly. That much was true. Bo could probably slide back into a low-level beat gig with the Sonoran Times. From there, if she really buckled down, she could work her way up to Phoenix one day. Her dream job was investigative journalism. And that didn't exist in small-town U.S.A. If you wanted to suss out edgy stories and dig at the truth, you had to live where things weren't so... *easy*. Sure, Maplewood had its share of high-drama, but things like murder and tragedy only happened every several years. If she was *lucky*.

Then again, her mind flicked back to the year before. Her sister's plane crash. The missing tourist. She squashed those exceptions and set her jaw.

"Well, there's no denying that you can do better," Keegan agreed, to Bo's surprised. He turned to the counter and grabbed the bottle of wine, filling their glasses and easing onto the bench seat across from her.

Bo loved Keegan's one-room cabin. It was like living in *Little House on the Prairie*. The smells of firewood and roasted coffee beans wrapped them up like a scarf. In the mornings, when Bo was around, a hint of aftershave filled the space, which made her want desperately to snuggle under a thick wool blanket. Sometimes, when they both had the day off, they would do just that. They would pop popcorn and sip from mugs of hot cocoa and duck under a blanket together, talking about their highlights and lowlights from the week. The former always being any dates they sneaked in. The latter being any time during the days when they had to be apart.

And, Keegan was a clean person. Bo loved this about him as much as she loved his sense of adventure and his good looks.

"You think I can do better?"

"You can do whatever you want, Bo. You're crazy smart. You're sexy as all get-out."

Bo flushed and rolled her eyes, smiling to herself. "I hate it when you use that word."

"I can't think of another word that fits you."

"Pretty?"

"You're more than pretty, Roberta Delaney."

Again, she rolled her eyes. "I hate it when you call me that, too."

"Well, gosh, Bo. You hate the word 'sexy.' You hate your real name. You hate your job—"

"I said I liked it!" She reached across the table and play-punched him in the chest.

He pretended to be wounded, rubbing the spot as he pushed her wine glass closer to her and sipped from his own. "Are you serious?"

"About what?"

"About moving to Tucson."

"Yes, Keegan. I am." Her face turned somber, and she ran her tongue across her lips.

"The grass is always greener, huh?" Keegan's voice took on a cutting edge. He crossed his arms over his chest and leaned away from the table.

Bo frowned. "What's that supposed to mean?"

"It's never enough for you. You moved off the mountain the minute you graduated and then bounced around from place to place. You couldn't settle down if your life depended on it, Bo. Why not?"

She swallowed at the accusation, her face draining of color and blood settling in her throat, preventing her from answering.

Bo did not understand why she couldn't settle down. She supposed it began when she ran away after high school. She and Keegan had something going on, but she never wanted to be *that* girl. The one who fell in love at sixteen and turned up to graduation pregnant and wearing a tinny nickel engagement ring around her swollen finger.

So she ran.

And kept on running until she wound up back in Maplewood to help her sister run the Wood Smoke Lodge. Bumping into Keegan again felt good. And she'd even discovered that she might like to settle with him.

But it had been several months now that they were working through an adult relationship and not once had he mentioned marriage. In fact, he'd slammed it. Making slights at other people who married their high school sweethearts and never made much of their lives. Making digs on people who hung all their happiness on romance.

"I would settle down," she answered quietly.

Keegan made a scoffing sound and pushed up from the table. He didn't ask, so she didn't finish her sentence. Instead, she grabbed her satchel from the chair by the front door and stormed out.

Slumped in her car, Bo turned the key in the ignition and muttered the rest of what she would've said. A lame, girlish reply. But a reply that Keegan Flanagan would never get the privilege to hear.

I'd settle down all right. With you.

Chapter 2

Keegan Flanagan had pride. And a demanding job. And an increasingly bored father who was on the brink of retirement and looking for a golf buddy.

All that had to be enough to distract him from another break-up with Roberta Delaney. *Was it a break-up?*

On the drive to work the next morning, he gave Alan a ring. Alan was Bo's brother and a friend of Keegan's. Not a close friend, necessarily, but close enough to call once in a while. Closer a friend than Keegan's own brothers, in fact. And even closer a friend than Keegan's father—the former mayor of Maplewood who'd been forced to "retire" from his term early for incompetency.

Keegan shook his shame like a late spring frost that just wouldn't lift.

"Hey, man. What's up?"

"Alan, how ya been doing?" Keegan let his mountain accent out and leaned back in his truck as he set cruise control on the narrow lane Maplewood called a highway.

"Getting ready for the Cook-Off. We're hosting this year, you know."

Alan and the other Delaney son, Robbie, owned and operated an outdoor bar called the BARn. It was connected to their parents' apple orchard and had quickly become the venue du jour for anything Maplewood needed.

"Jeez, that's coming up soon, right?" Keegan frowned, trying to remember the date.

Alan answered, "Two weeks. Macaroni and Cheese. I love mac 'n' cheese, but doesn't it seem sort of lame to you?"

Keegan laughed. "Naw. It'll be fine." He silently swore and made a mental note to dig up a recipe he could pull together. His mother would be no help. She was too busy running her real estate "empire" and bossing around her husband. Keegan briefly considered the ethics of buying a box of instant mac before Alan asked why he was calling.

"Honestly, Alan, I know you don't want me to drag you into this, but I'm calling about Bo."

A tsking sound made its way through Keegan's earpiece. "I don't get involved in any of my sisters' romantic affairs and *especially* not Roberta's and *specifically* not when it involves one of my high school buddies."

"It's not about our relationship, Alan. Hear me out."

Instead of sighing, Alan's voice turned panicky. "Is she okay? Did she get hurt?"

"No, no. Nothing like that. She's safe," Keegan assured him, reminding himself how protective brothers could be. Especially when it concerned the wild-child of the family. Pretty much every member of the Delaney brood and most of the mountain were just waiting for the other shoe to drop with Bo. She could be reckless. It's what he loved about her, really.

"Then what?" Alan's voice turned irritated, so Keegan got to the point.

"She says she's leaving Maplewood and moving back to Tucson. Is that true, Al?"

"Roberta threatens to move off the mountain every weekend. What happened? Did the Last Chance close an hour early on Saturday?"

If she weren't his girlfriend—or even ex-girlfriend—Keegan would have laughed. Bo enjoyed spending her Saturday evenings at the only watering hole in town, but she wasn't a drinker. Mostly just a watcher. A people watcher. Keegan supposed that sort of thing came with the job. Journalists had to be where the drama broke out. A bar was her best chance.

"Well, she seems serious. Says she wants to move up in the world. Get a better writing gig."

Alan scoffed. "She *had* a better writing gig. She wrote for the *Sonoran*, didn't she? Got the boot, didn't she? If she wants a better job then she has to prove her worth *somewhere*. She'd be dumb to uproot again. No one wants an employee who scans the classifieds at work. Even if *she's* the one writing them."

Alan laughed at his own joke and reminded Keegan again about the cook-out before they said their goodbyes.

As he parked his truck in the back lot of the station, Keegan thought about Alan's words and found himself in agreement. But still, something nagged at him. Something that Bo didn't quite *say* but implied. It was in her eyes. The way she forced herself to keep her gaze off of him. The sadness in her suggestion.

Maybe Bo *didn't* want to leave town. Sure, she'd like to have hotter stories on a more regular basis. But maybe she wanted to stay, and she just needed a good reason.

If only Keegan or Alan had the slightest clue about that reason.

KEEGAN HAD ONLY JUST clocked in and greeted his partner, when Dispatch came over the radio.

"Apache County Sheriff's Department, we have callers advising of an endangered hiking party out past Zick Ranch Road."

Keegan grabbed his radio first. "Go ahead, Dispatch."

"Caller advises that a hiker from their party left the campsite to use the restroom yesterday at approximately twenty-three hundred hours. Has yet to return. Over."

"When did the call come in?" Keegan asked, alarm prickling up his spine. Missing hikers were becoming a plague on the mountain, and nine times out of ten it was a party of tourists. He blew out a sigh as dispatch gave him all the pertinent information available.

The call had only recently come through, and so Keegan and another ranger, Dirk Smith, jumped in an SUV and punched the sirens before tearing off toward one of the more obscure hiking trails on the mountain.

It was early for hiking and camping in or near Maplewood. Snow still capped the peaks and the skiing season stayed open for another two weeks, yet. Just in time for Maplewood to turn over from winter guests to spring and summer tourism. The Ranger's Round-up was, in fact, the very beginning of the true tourist season. By late April, the area could count on more warm days than cold—usually.

But not this year. This year, winter had clung to the mountaintop with desperation.

Dirk read Keegan's mind. "Who's hiking this time of year? Hunting party, maybe?"

"Too early. We're a few weeks off turkey season, at least."

"Stupid tourists, no doubt."

Keegan thought about Bo and a few of the articles she'd written the year before. It was just after she had returned to the mountain and was feeling the summer-time blues of being a local in a tourist town. He liked that side of her. He could relate. Tourists, though crucial to the economy, were law enforcement's worst offenders.

Protocol on missing persons in Apache County varied from case to case. Outside of camping or hiking, at least twenty-four hours must pass before anyone can open a formal investigation. But when a camper or hiker went missing overnight, on-duty search and rescue rangers responded immediately as the station put together a formalized plan and team. Out in the elements, anything could happen.

As soon as they arrived, Keegan off-loaded his four-wheeler from the trailer and sped toward the approximate campsite.

Within minutes, he'd arrived to find a small party shivering by a weak fire.

"Howdy!" Keegan called as he jumped off his ride and jogged up the hill toward the group. "County rangers. Here to assist." He pulled out a notepad and began taking down information while the second ranger began driving in circles out from the campsite.

Two men and one woman huddled together, clad in every article of clothing they'd brought. Keegan spared them the lecture and instead inquired about their reason for camping and jotted a timeline of events.

Shauna and Steve Watson and Devin and Cari Peters of Mesa, Arizona. Couples' camping trip. On a whim. Wanted to escape the Phoenix heat. Cari was the one missing. Devin told Keegan she'd had to go to the bathroom just before bedtime.

"Any reason you didn't join her?" Keegan asked, keeping his voice even. Devin pushed his palms into his eye sockets and three more ATVs of rangers and law enforcement personnel pulled up to a stop at the campground.

"I figured she wasn't going far. I set the lantern outside the tent," Devin answered, meekly.

Other officers waited patiently as Keegan gave them curt directions on what to do. Helicopters would need to get set. It was nearly nine in the morning. She'd been gone for too long by now.

"You were already asleep?" Keegan pressed, glancing around the stricken, ruddy faces.

Devin nodded, ashamed. "Or I fell asleep soon after. I didn't realize she was gone until we called you guys. This morning." The man looked down and Keegan nodded. "We'll have to take you three into the station for further questions soon. Stay put."

Keegan radioed the station with his updates. The whole situation was bizarre. He prayed this was nothing more than a woman who lost her way.

Chapter 3

RECKLESS HIKING HAS DIRE CONSE-QUENCES: PHOENIX TOURIST MISSING IN MOUNTAINS

By Bo Delaney, *Mountain Times*

ZICK'S RANCH BLUFFS—At just after eight o'clock this morning, a hiking party called the Apache County Sheriff's Office to report that one of their own had been missing from their campsite for nearly ten hours.

The missing woman is Mesa native Cari Peters. She is five feet, four inches tall, brown-haired, and weighs approximately 155 pounds. She was last seen at the campsite about one mile south of the trailhead.

According to initial reports, Peters may or may not have been imbibing. Evidence of foul play is being considered.

Sheriff's Ranger Keegan Flanagan was first to respond to the call and, initially found no hint of wrongdoing. However, something isn't sitting right with the Sheriff's Department, particularly considering the untimely hiking vacation and the husband's evasive behavior.

A team of search and rescue rangers continues to canvass the area. Those willing to volunteer are asked to report to the search headquarters at the Zick Ranch Bluff Trailhead off of Zick Ranch Road and Zick Bluff Road.

Bo Delaney is an investigative reporter for the Mountain Times, covering local and late-breaking news around the mountain and in Maplewood.

"BO, WHAT ARE YOU *doing*?"

Keegan's voice was low and cold through the phone. With her hand over the receiver, she snapped her work laptop shut and stepped out onto the back deck of the *Mountain Times* offices.

"What are you talking about, Keegan?" Her mind swirled. She thought they had broken up. Why call now?

"The article you wrote. It's borderline gossip. How did you get that information, anyway?"

A grin formed on her mouth, but she forced it down to answer him calmly. "I'm a reporter. And when there's news, I report it. Especially something like this."

"Bo," Keegan hissed into the line. "I don't understand your angle. This is serious. Not some big city exposé on dumb tourists. What are you going for? Exploitation?"

She could practically hear him shake his head in disappointment. Her heart sank. "No. Jeez, Keegan. The department put out a press release. It literally *is* my job to inform the public."

"I thought you were going to go inform the *Tucson* public."

"Well, not yet. I figured you'd appreciate that I found something to cover while I was still here?" Her heart thudded in her chest and she pressed the phone closer to her ear, waiting for him to make a move. Anything.

"If you're going to cover mountain news, then at least do it well. What you wrote sounded like something that gossip rag reporter out of Lowell would string together. You are better than that."

A dial tone took the place of Keegan's harsh voice, and Bo all but crumpled to the ground. His words stung for two reasons. One, because they came from *him*, the man she loved. Trusted, even. And, two, because they were true.

But Bo did not crumple to the ground. She wasn't the type. Instead, she shoved her phone into the back pocket of her jeans and tore out of the office and to the trailhead.

After all, Keegan was right. She could do better. Especially better than Annabelle Jackson of the Lowell Gazette.

"I'M LOOKING FOR KEEGAN Flanagan." She'd brought her hand-recorder and a palm-sized notebook with a golf pencil, all shoved into the pocket of an oversized sweatshirt hoodie

THE RANGER'S MOUNTAIN BRIDE 19

that read across the front *DON'T HASSLE ME. I'M LOCAL* in fading yellow letters.

The woman behind the folding table studied Bo. Bo studied her back. She looked familiar. Probably someone her family knew. Older—mid-sixties. She wore a rubber visor and a windbreaker with matching windbreaker pants. She needed them, too, because the breeze from in town turned into full-blown gusts up at the trailhead.

"He's at the campsite, dear," the woman answered. "If you're volunteering, we ask that you sign in and find a buddy. No one searches alone. That's the rule." The woman offered Bo a warm smile as she held up a clipboard and a pen.

Bo began to shake her head, but Keegan's words pressed down on her heart. So, too, did something she learned in college. Good journalists report the news. Great journalists live it.

She scanned the area, her eyes falling on a rigid-looking elderly man in Wranglers and a neatly tucked button down. A cowboy hat stood sentinel atop his head, and his hands were pressed tightly into his front pockets.

"Are you waiting for a volunteer partner?" Bo asked him, as she took the clipboard and scrawled down her name and phone number.

"Yes, ma'am," he replied. For someone north of sixty, he was sharp and alert. Ready to get to work. Good, old-fashioned Maplewood stock. "I been tryin' to get this here woman to join me, but she claims she has to stay put." He took his hat off and waved it respectfully toward the woman at the table and, then, much to both women's surprise, he winked at her.

Bo smiled at this small-town flirtation and then slapped on her nametag and picked up a bottle of water from the cooler to the right of the table.

"I could always man the table if you two want to take off," she said as she took a swig of water and eyed the blushing woman.

"No, no. I'm assigned to stay here. He can wait for me or come back later," she answered, suddenly stoic.

The gentleman nodded. "I'll come back, then."

Bo felt her stomach lurch a little with disappointment. Maybe she wasn't the only one with issues in the romance department.

THEY'D WALKED HALF a mile together, Bo and Roger, and in that short time, discovered nothing new regarding the missing hiker (although, they wouldn't discover anything new since they'd walked toward the campsite and not yet fanned out as the other volunteers had).

Roger was good at small talk, asking Bo a little about herself. They'd learned their families had crossed paths in different ways. His children and grandchildren attended Maplewood High on either side of the Delaney kids. And he knew Bo's dad well from bartering livestock and produce through the years. Roger had lost his wife years earlier in an unfortunate car accident but claimed he was ready for romance again. Bo believed him.

Once they arrived at the campsite, Roger caught sight of Keegan first and greeted him warmly, apparently being familiar

THE RANGER'S MOUNTAIN BRIDE 21

with all the law enforcement. It seemed like old men were always like that—casual friends with the law.

Over Roger's head, Keegan spotted Bo and frowned. She glared back until Roger wandered over to another ranger.

"What are you doing here, Bo?"

She shrugged, her eyebrows arched, and spit her reply. "Helping, actually."

He studied her, suspicious. "You're not here to get the gossip?"

"Well, yes. I'm going to report. But I heard what you said."

"And what was that?"

Bo smirked. "I could do a better job."

Keegan considered this and glanced around. "Are you and Roger partners?"

She looked over at the old man and realized, for the first time, that he wore no ring on his left finger. "I think he'd rather be partners with the woman working your headquarters down there." She jutted her chin off in the direction of the trailhead.

Keegan laughed. "Yeah, Roger is a bit of a hound, actually."

Bo squinted through the early morning light. "*That* guy?"

"Oh, yeah. I guess you haven't been back in town long enough to hear the stories. Anyway..." Keegan ran a hand through his hair and offered a small grin.

"I'm here to help. With or without Roger, I guess."

"In that case, you can team up with me. I was just about to take off on another drive east with Benson, but maybe he can take Roger, instead."

Bo's eyes lit up. "That's great. What is your mission?"

Keegan shouted a command to Benson and waved Bo toward his four-wheeler. "All we're doing is trying to find this woman. Simple as that."

She nodded and jumped on the back of the ATV. As it roared to life, Bo wrapped her arms around Keegan's waist and pressed the side of her face into his back. Once they took off down the mountain, the sound of helicopter blades beating the air above them kept her from asking the one question that was burning a hole in her reporter's notebook.

Chapter 4

As soon as she'd shown up, a question formed on Keegan's mind. But he couldn't ask. Not yet.

First work, then play.

That was exactly how Bo had always wanted it, too. She put her career above their relationship. So he may as well do the same.

Information on the events surrounding the Peters disappearance was still limited. Keegan could not understand how the husband did not wake up once in the night looking for his wife. If Keegan were married—even if he wasn't; if it were Bo who went missing—he'd probably naturally wake up. Camping in the cold mountains was no recipe for a good night's sleep. Undoubtedly the man would have stirred from a frigid sleep looking for the comfort of a warm body.

Then again, for all the husband knew, Peters had returned to their tent in the night and possibly left again early in the morning for another restroom break. If she had left before dawn broke, then it was a probable theory. Disoriented by the cold and the dark, she likely could have taken a wrong turn just a short distance from the tent. And, as any search and rescue ranger knew, wrong turns grew exponentially in the middle of a dark forest.

Still, where was the husband during it all?

They careened around rock formations and through thickly wooded thatches of the mountain. Within five minutes, the ATV had covered almost two miles and was far enough away from the chopping noise of the 'copters, which had spanned out in other directions. By now, Keegan and Bo could hear each other well enough. In the relative silence, he felt himself focus on Bo's body against his and her arms around his abdomen.

"What did you find out from the press release?" Keegan shouted over his shoulder to thwart the distraction of their too-close contact.

Bo's mouth drew near to his ear. "All they said was that she left the campsite last night, and the group reported her missing this morning!"

He nodded and turned his attention back to the road, his eyes scanning efficiently through damp oak trunks and blooming aspens. Spring resulted in a raw, dewy aftermath of foliage.

As Keegan looked ahead, navigating an especially narrow thoroughfare between two Douglas fir trees, Bo shouted into his ear and tugged hard on his sides. "Keegan! Look!"

A HIDDEN RAVINE RAN along their tracks, and just below the lip, Bo—and now Keegan—could spot something that was not a branch or a rock, not flora or fauna. Rather, it was human.

Keegan had been in this position many times in his career. And though he knew that in her role as a reporter, Bo was no stranger to horror, he refused to let her be the one to come upon an unsightly scene first.

"Stay here," he commanded sharply, pressing a hand on her shoulder as he dismounted the four-wheeler and pulled his radio off his chest. Bo, for once in her life, listened, and he called for back-up before jogging down to the ravine.

There, lying face down along the inside slope of a relatively shallow ditch, was a brown-haired woman clad in thermal underwear, UGG-style boots, and a puffy sweatshirt.

He couldn't help himself. He shouted up to Bo. "It's her! I think it's her!"

Bo dashed down next to him as Keegan lifted the woman's limp wrist and pressed his fingers to the inside. Bo jumped down to the far end, near the woman's head and stared at Keegan as he waited, his own heart throbbing with fear.

After nearly a moment too long, he felt it. A faint pulsating. "She's alive," he whispered before taking up his radio and updating the incoming rangers and emergency personnel.

"Cari?" Bo spoke softly into the woman's ear, careful not to move her head as per Keegan's directions.

"Keep talking to her Bo," he added.

"Cari, can you hear me? You're okay, Cari. My name is Roberta. We're here to help you, Cari."

Keegan's heartbeat ebbed and settled into a comfortable rhythm as a second ATV peeled up the hill and slammed to a stop just behind Keegan's.

"Down here!" Keegan shouted as a man with a medic bag jogged down and took control of assessing her vitals.

Reluctantly, Bo backed off and joined Keegan at the four-wheeler as he called in a third update. She leaned into the vehicle and watched the growing team of paramedics position Cari onto a stretcher and into a trailer by which to transport her out of the woods. By then, she was awake, aware, and even talking. She was dehydrated, it appeared, and had tripped and fallen down the hillside sometime earlier that morning.

The husband's theory was correct, if still unsettling.

Bo said as much. "What a weird story," she said to Keegan.

He nodded and saw her shiver. Wrapping an arm around her shoulders, Keegan felt the question bubble back up to his mind, taking the place of his concern over the missing tourist.

"So..." he began, awkward as a teenage boy on his first date. "What do you think, Bo?"

Chapter 5

"Well," she started, sighing into his shoulder. "I think there's more to the story, obviously. And I intend to get to the bottom of it. Think you can get me access to the husband under false pretenses?"

Keegan frowned at her and dropped his arm. "No."

Bo felt her cheeks flush. She'd crossed a line. She often did. It was like a bad habit. Lifting her finger to her mouth, she gnawed on a hangnail and looked up from beneath her lashes at him. "Hm?" Dropping her hand, she shook her head. "I'm sorry. You're right. Unprofessional. Inappropriate. I would not want to compromise your job or anything."

A cold chuckle blew from his mouth and Keegan turned away to straddle the quad and rev the engine. "No," he repeated nodding his head for her to jump on behind him.

Confused, Bo pressed on with her apology. "I mean, Keegan, I'm sorry I even asked. But don't you think it's weird that she was drunk in the morning and wandered off? Plus her husband—what a lame-o for not looking harder. She wasn't *that* far from the campsite and—"

"Bo," Keegan cut her off before pulling away. "This isn't about you finding a juicy news story. I wasn't asking about that."

"Then what were you asking about? I mean, this is literally what we are here to do—find the woman. We found her, but it was weird, right?"

"Yeah, it was unfortunate. There are lots of news stories like hers. Or theirs. Where the couple doesn't communicate, for example." He killed the engine and turned to face her. "If you go to Tucson, you'll find your share of sad stories like this one. Wobbly marriages. Sick folks. People who abuse drugs and drink. And people who make dumb choices like taking a hiking trip in the dead of cold. It all boils down to humanity, right? And humans are no different in a small town than in a big city. There just happens to be more of them."

Bo blinked and glanced off to where they'd found the poor lady, nearly frost-bitten and entirely delirious. Technically, Keegan was right. If she lived in Tucson or Phoenix and worked her way up to the more serious beats, then stories like this would become old news—not wild adventures.

Or would they?

"I can't help it. I'm interested in other people—how they live, what they see, what they do. I want to solve mysteries and I want to write. There are only so many stories in Maplewood, Keegan."

He turned back around and started the engine again. "I guess you don't know Maplewood," he called over his shoulder.

She shook her head as she wrapped her arms around his waist, this time with less enthusiasm. Keegan pressed the gas and flipped around to return them to the trailhead. Bo thought back to the origin of their conversation. "Keegan, what did you mean?" she hollered.

"When?"

THE RANGER'S MOUNTAIN BRIDE

"When you asked what I thought?"

She felt him shake his head above before he answered. "I meant between you and me. What are we doing?" he shouted back, craning his neck to catch her expression quickly before turning his head again.

"Well, that's up to you!" she called back.

He didn't answer, and it was not until they returned to the search headquarters and Keegan had caught up with the rangers that she had another chance to talk to him.

"I'm heading back to the station to write up my report. You might as well come with me, since you were first on scene, too. Sound good?" Keegan stared daggers at her before Bo nodded her head sheepishly.

If it was a story she wanted, it was a story she would get.

"WHAT IS 'UP TO ME'?" he asked as they slid into the front seat of his truck in tandem.

"Us, I mean. Our future. Our present. Whatever our status is," she answered earnestly.

"How can you say that now? You emphasized that you're moving to Tucson. You know darn well I'm staying here, so..."

A breeze curled around the trees and blew in her cracked window. She pressed the automatic button to close it.

"Keegan, listen. It's not like I'm leaving yet. Why don't we just... why don't we just see where things go the next couple weeks, okay? Go back to old times until the dust settles."

He slowed to a stop at an empty four-way intersection and looked over to her. "What do you mean? Keep dating? Despite your leaving?"

"I'm not leaving yet. Let's just see. Maybe something will change." She folded her arms across her chest and smirked inwardly. She had an idea. Maybe this would work.

And it did.

"No. I need commitment, Bo."

Chapter 6

Keegan wasn't into games, and if that's where Bo was going, then he was putting a stop to it.

Though, she was more than satisfied with his answer; pleased even. In fact, the whole ride back to the station she chatted gleefully about her suppositions regarding the missing woman. Ideas she had for his cabin. Her summer plans.

Whatever he'd said was exactly what she needed to hear, apparently.

Now, all Keegan had to worry about was what to cook for the Ranger Round-up.

PHOENIX TOURIST FOUND ALIVE, SAFE

By Bo Delaney, *Mountain Times*

ZICK'S RANCH BLUFFS—Within three hours of the search and rescue efforts, Mesa native Cari Peters was found alive in a ravine less than two miles east of the campsite.

Ranger Keegan Flanagan of the Apache County Sheriff's Search and Rescue Unit was first on the scene and identified the woman from beneath his position along a clearing.

According to an exclusive interview with Mrs. Peters and her camping party with the *Mountain Times*, the disappearance came on the heels of a long and late night and a lack of preparation on behalf of the hikers.

Peters and the others in the party have given the *Times* permission to publish this article as a cautionary tale and a way to inform mountain visitors about the dangers of misunderstanding climate considerations and regional nuances of recreation on the mountain.

According to the hikers, they drove to Maplewood around lunchtime on the Thursday before Peters went missing. The party intended to hike Zick Ranch Bluffs until sundown and then establish a base camp by approximately seven o'clock in the evening.

Worn down from carrying their backpacks, they settled for the evening and had a barbecue. In the course of grilling hot dogs for an easy supper, the group decided to stay up and chat until the late hours of the evening.

At eleven o'clock, the foursome called it a night and went to their separate tents to catch enough shuteye

THE RANGER'S MOUNTAIN BRIDE

to tide them over for a morning hike before returning down to the valley.

Soon after settling into their sleeping bags, Peters informed her husband she needed to use the restroom but would return briefly.

Though Peters' husband had already fallen asleep in that short window, he therefore assumed she may have disappeared as early as eleven in the evening. In fact Peters *did* return to the tent, snuggling up to her husband to shake the chill and an increasingly achy feeling.

What no one realized was that Peters had come down with an upper respiratory tract infection. She assumed the cold was from the weather, not a fever, and fitfully shivered the whole night through.

Unable to sleep at all, she left the tent a second time before dawn, shakily shuffling through the trees to try to find a discreet location again.

Moments turned to minutes, and minutes turned to hours before she became lost and hopeless, tripping over a ropy oak root and sailing head first into a shallow ditch. The fall coupled with her lack of sleep and growing ailment knocked her unconscious. Dehydration and the fever kept her that way for hours until help arrived.

Back at the campsite, thanks to the consumption of a few adult beverages, Peters' husband was dead asleep, unaware that his wife was sick and oblivious that she had wandered off. When he awoke in the morning, panic struck him—and guilt. He was angry with himself for his own choices and scared for his wife. So scared, in fact, that his first instinct was to call 911—a vital decision. But Devin Peters did not stop there. He took it upon himself to search the immediate area, screaming out for his beloved wife and running laps to find her.

Crushed by his inability to save the love of his life, he begged law enforcement officials to allow him to assist in the search. Devin Peters rode along the back of a four-wheeler, blowing a whistle and crying out for Cari until news came that she was inadvertently hiding in plain sight—so close to the camp.

The couple's reunion at the hospital was something out of a romance novel—happy tears and embraces all around.

Cari Peters and her husband would, however, want tourists to learn one thing from their mistakes: trust the news and the weather forecast. It's important that visitors always consider the Farmer's Almanac before planning any off-season camping trips or hikes. After all, spring in Maplewood is a fickle mistress.

Bo Delaney is an investigative reporter for the Mountain Times, covering local and late-breaking news around the mountain and in Maplewood.

KEEGAN LAID THE NEWSPAPER across his oak kitchen table and took a swig from the hot cocoa Bo had warmed for them. She was curled up in the armchair near his fireplace, sipping through a blanket of marshmallows.

"It's a great piece, Bo." He meant it. She treated the conundrum with gravity and drama but also with tact.

"Thank you. I suppose I learned a lot from this one."

"Oh?" he asked, joining her in the adjacent armchair as though they were a regular Holmes and Watson.

"I guess I like happy endings." Her eyes blazed with flames from the fire.

Keegan's pulse quickened, and he set his hot cocoa on a crochet coaster on the side table, careful to keep from splashing any hot liquid onto the wood. "Come over here, you," he directed Bo, who flashed a sweet grin and did as she was told, following his example of cradling her mug on a matching coaster.

She padded the short distance to his chair, which stood closer to the fire. He opened his arms and moved to the far corner of the oversized chair, allowing her to tuck herself into the nook he made for her.

"I love this. Being here with you. Couldn't ask for a more perfect date night." She sighed contentedly and laid her head on his chest.

"If that's true, then how could you move away?"

As though a chill coursed down the chimney and snuck past the fire, Bo shivered and pushed up from her brief reprieve. "Why do you have to do that?"

"Do what?" he asked, genuinely confused.

"Spoil a nice moment? I said I loved this, and you turned it into an argument." Despite what she was saying, Bo's voice was soft and curious rather than scolding or accusatory.

For once in their relationship, he didn't have a quip or a terse reply. He stared back at her. "I'm not sure."

"You want me to stay, I get that. And, honestly Keegan, I *want* to stay."

"That's exactly why I spoiled the nice moment. I want to have a lifetime of them, and if we can't come to an agreement now, then I can't—"

"Can't what?" Bo cut him off at the pass, repositioning herself on her small real estate and pinning him with a glare the likes of which he'd never seen. "Can't commit?"

"That's not what I was going to say."

"Then what were you going to say, Keegan? You're not willing to compromise? To move with me? Or let me try things out?"

"Exactly, Bo. It's not about moving, though. It's the fact that I refuse to have a long-distance relationship. I see what distance of any kind does to a marriage and I refuse to set myself up for unhappiness." Keegan shut his mouth before he went too far. It was one thing to remind her he wanted to stay in town. It was another to reveal his deepest darkest fears. She didn't need to hear them or carry them. She wouldn't understand, anyway. Bo came from a perfect family with parents

THE RANGER'S MOUNTAIN BRIDE 37

who loved each other. A husband and wife who put each other ahead of their careers or anything else.

But Bo caught onto something he'd said. He could see it in her eyes. "What?" he pressed, leaning into the far arm.

"Marriage?"

His eyes dancing circles trying to understand her question but he failed. "What?" he asked, again.

"You are worried about putting a strain on marriage. Is that something you want in life? To get married?"

"Bo, now's not the time. Okay? What you and I have works. There is no reason to change anything for any reason."

The flames began to turn a cool blue behind them, and the once-sturdy logs now glowed orange.

She bit down on her lip then drew a finger to her mouth and nibbled. "Okay," she answered, slowly.

One of Keegan's eyebrows lifted in disbelief.

"Okay, what?"

"You want me to stay. You don't want to talk marriage. You just want things to be like they are."

"Yes..." he began, growing more tense rather than less.

"You want those things, and I want one thing."

"What's that?" Keegan felt his pace quicken. He and Bo weren't the type of couple to make little bets or deals. They didn't have any formal arrangement. Everything was cool and casual. So what could she want?

"I want unconditional press access."

"What?" he asked, rubbing his hand up the back of his neck.

"Make it worth my while. When there's a hot case—a missing hiker, for example, or a shoplifting mystery—I want a tip."

"You can't ask me to favor you, Bo. It's unethical."

"No, no. I don't want you to favor me, and I don't want you to break any laws or ethical codes. I just want you to do whatever is in your power to grant the *Mountain Times* the earliest possible access. You're a ranger. You see the action first. If you are unwilling to make a compromise for me, then this is the least you can do. Give yourself over to me. Let me get more behind-the-scenes. Treat me like I'm important."

He dropped his hand from the back of his head and covered hers with it, staring deeply into her eyes. This was exactly why they weren't ready for the marriage talk. Because to Bo, career leverage was just as sweet as a honeymoon would ever be.

And he loved it about her.

"Deal," he answered firmly. And with that, Keegan cupped her face in his hands and pulled her to him before pressing his lips onto hers.

She let him linger there for only a moment before pulling her face away—her eyes closed—, tucking her head into the crook of his neck, and whispering back, "Deal."

Chapter 7

"That sounds like a weird agreement."

When Bo returned to Mary's lodge the night before, her sister was half asleep in the love seat. Bo nudged her awake and told her she'd better just stay the night rather than drive home.

Mary agreed, and together the sisters trudged up to bed in Bo's room—the room at the end of the second-floor hall that, for ten years, belonged to Bo's determined youngest sister as she worked hard to bring the mountain lodge back to life. Mary had moved out only the previous October, when Bo agreed to move in as the overnight attendant, allowing Mary to follow her personal dreams for once.

Come morning, the coffee machine beeped to life, and the two women chatted at the front desk over steaming mugs as a few guests checked in and out and asked little questions here and there.

Springtime was not the busiest season for any bed-and-breakfast, hotel, motel, or otherwise on the mountain. However, ever since Mary reinvigorated the place with a makeover and a few well-timed events, it had become the go-to hub for locals and tourists alike. If you needed charming and rustic accommodation or wanted to have a big party, the Wood Smoke Lodge was the only option in Maplewood.

A fire roared in the cavernous great room behind them, warming the chilly space and adding irresistible ambience to the exposed wood beam ceilings and leather furnishings.

"Why do you say weird? He got something, I got something, right?"

"Bo, have a little self-respect. He literally got everything he wanted, and all you get is a promise that he'll let you know when something happens in town? You're already good enough at sussing out drama. Why do you need him to do it?"

Mary's question was valid, if heartbreaking. "I want him to take my career seriously."

"He takes your career seriously. Listen, Bo, everyone loves Keegan. He's a great guy. Hardworking and handsome. But, he loves his job as much as you love yours. I think it's fair of us to assume he knows how much your work matters." The petite, chestnut-haired woman shrugged and pulled out a bottle of furniture polish and a rag from the bottom shelf behind the desk.

Bo considered what she said, frowning deeply as she sipped at the too-sweet liquid. "Did you add sugar to mine, too?"

"Just a little," Mary answered, squirting oil onto the rag and working it across the waxen wooden surface.

"I hate sugar in my coffee." Bo left Mary and went to the kitchen to dump the cup, rinse out the little crystalline beads that clung to the lip, and pour herself a fresh mug just the way she liked it: black, no sugar.

Returning to the desk, Bo grabbed the old-fashioned guest log to check the stats for the night before and glimpse ahead at who was checking out in the next hour.

THE RANGER'S MOUNTAIN BRIDE 41

"Is it the Lodge?" Mary asked meekly, as she finished oiling and capped the bottle.

"Is what the Lodge?" Bo replied, highlighting the recently departed guests.

"Is that what you hate about Maplewood? Working here for me in your spare time? Living here?"

Bo couldn't deal with Mary's insecurities right then. "What I hate about Maplewood is that I will never be what I want to be here."

There. She'd said it. Finally, and at last.

Mary's face fell and her eyebrows sank down. "What? What do you mean?"

Shaking her head, Bo's eyes welled up. "I don't hate Maplewood, Mare. Actually, I love it. I love the seasons and I love being near you and Mom and Dad."

"Then what's going on with you, sis?"

"Mary, you know, I just want a reason to be here. Something more than my roots, honestly. Something to say when people ask why I came back. Some kind of answer when I ask myself why I couldn't make it work in Tucson or Vegas or Nashville."

Mary hopped onto her barstool and laced her fingers together on top of the desk. "You have your job at the paper."

"Mary, come on. Most of what I write about is crap like the stupid Ranger Round-up. Or which obscure hot-air balloon people are joining us for the annual hot-air balloon festival. The best average piece I get to cover is the drama from the monthly town council meetings."

"Well, you just did two write-ups on that missing tourist," Mary reasoned.

"Yeah, but I want to write pieces like that every single day. That's why I asked Keegan for help."

"You want human interest stories that are a little more human, huh?"

Bo stared back at her little sister, amazed at the wisdom such a little pip like Mary could offer. She let out a small laugh. "Yeah, that's probably true. I want connections. Not just events."

"And you want Keegan to propose."

Caught entirely off guard, Bo shook her head violently. "No, no, no. I don't want to get married. No, thank you. Commitment, yes. Compromise? Always. Not vows. No, thank you."

"I call bull," Mary replied, crossing her arms over her flannel shirt.

"Call bull all you want. I don't need a wedding to be happy."

"Oh right, you value people, not parties, huh?"

At that, Bo cracked a grin.

Mary went on. "See, Bo, what you're forgetting is that people put on 'events' and 'parties' for darn good reasons. It's how we connect, you know. I think I have an idea for you."

"What?" Bo asked, chewing on her thumbnail.

"A challenge, if you will."

"Okay..." Bo's eyes lit up, and she tucked her hands into her back pockets. "Go on."

"Forget the deal with Keegan. Forget Keegan, if you have to. Instead, I want you to find three local events and do a write-up on someone connected to each one." Mary's eyes glimmered with the coziness of a small-town innkeeper.

"I literally just told you no more *events*."

"You're not hearing me, girl. I said report on *someone* connected with the events. You fulfill your job—and maybe you'll even do it well—" Mary chuckled at her lame joke; Bo fake punched her in the arm. "And, you'll satisfy your thirst for studying the human condition."

"Okay, so what if Keegan gives me some juicy crime tips?"

"Forget him. Focus on this. I mean jot down what he says if you feel so compelled. Follow up in your spare time. But for now, three people; three events."

Bo did, in fact, trust Mary with decisions about men. And life, even. Mary had patience. Mary had values. And both had paid off for her.

What did Bo have to lose? A lame deal with the boyfriend who refused to budge an inch?

"What if I don't succeed?" Bo asked Mary before bringing her finger to her mouth to chew on an errant hangnail.

"You know the answer to that," her sister replied.

Bo shrugged and chewed harder.

"Bo, if you can't come up with three good stories, then you're not a good writer."

"Okay, then. You're on," Bo answered.

Chapter 8

"Hey, Bo, it's me. Keegan. Obviously," Keegan cleared his throat awkwardly. He rarely left messages on Bo's voicemail, but he had made her a promise and intended to keep it. "Just got the green light to inform you that The Duces, you know—that corner gas station on the way out of town? Well, it was hit with a burglary last night. Cops have finished examining the scene, and the place is back open. I'm sure the clerk there would be happy to answer questions. They are actively searching for the perp. Anyway, call me back if you have questions."

He paused, pushing his hand through his hair. "Oh, and I have a favor to ask, Bo. Well, call me when you can. Okay. Bye, Bo."

Hanging up, Keegan returned his attention to a blank report on his desk. He and Dirk had been called out to deal with wild horses that kept terrorizing the Maplewood Little League baseball field.

For once in his career, Keegan could not focus on work. Too many things felt like a distraction. His stupid arrangement with Bo, the promotion his boss had hinted at weeks back and never mentioned again, and—most inane of all—the upcoming cook-out.

Keegan could flip a burger and burn a hot dog. But macaroni and cheese? Would they allow the boxed stuff?

Sighing to himself as he compulsively checked his cell for a text or incoming call from Bo, he closed out of the report and opted for a brisk walk around the station. He was feeling itchy.

And stressed.

So, as any good, self-sufficient man would do, he dealt with the one thing he could control the easiest: the cook-off.

"HELLO, MARGARET-JUNE Flanagan speaking."

"Aunt Marg, hey." Keegan breathed out and tucked his free hand into his uniform pocket as he leaned up against the back of the log-cabin building that housed the sheriff's department. The one woman he could count on with all things kitchen was his father's sister. The woman who raised him on the weekends, when he wanted to get out from under his household chaos.

"Is this my favorite nephew in the whole wide world?"

"You're not supposed to have favorites."

"And you're not supposed to be calling on the clock. What's up, Bubba?"

"I could ask you the same. 'Margaret-June Flanagan speaking'? Were you expecting someone?" he teased good naturedly.

She cackled into the phone, but her cackle quickly turned into a harsh cough. Finally, composing herself as Keegan frowned with worry, she answered, "The cook-out is less than two weeks off, Ranger. You should know that. I've been fielding calls at all hours of the day. *What time is it? Where is it? Who will be there? What will the weather be like? Will booze be served?* Heck, one person asked me if there would be a live pig roast. Which is a great idea for next year, in fact..." she trailed off and Keegan chuckled. "Your girlfriend's newspaper article did nothing to help me out," Margaret-June answered finally with a harrumph.

"Yeah, it was a little vague, but I guess she didn't have the information," he reasoned.

"She's a reporter. Isn't that her job?"

Shrugging, Keegan ignored the critical observation and sucked in a deep breath. "Aunt Marg, I need your help."

"Oh, boy. Here we go. Are you proposing? Tell me you aren't proposing to that girl."

"You mean to Bo?" Keegan pushed off the wall and started pacing.

"The reporter, yes. The girl you're dating but refuse to bring to my house. Tells me everything I need to know, Keegan."

A deep frown set across his face and he came up with a retort. "I haven't even been around your house lately, Aunt Marg."

"Well, then maybe I need to meet her."

"That's not why I'm calling," he replied, licking his lips and pulling the phone away momentarily to check to see if a text notification had come in yet. Nope.

"Well, how can I help, Bubba?"

"The Ranger's Round-up Cook-off." He didn't need to spell things out for his aunt. She was the coordinator for the event and knew that it was less than two weeks away. "I'm lost. Aunt Marg. Last year I got railed by my boss for not taking part, so this year I have to get my act together." He didn't add the talk of a promotion.

"Sorry, sonny. Not going to happen."

"What?" Keegan's jaw fell open. "But Marg—"

"That's *Aunt* Marg to you, and no can do, Ranger. As event coordinator, I am prohibited from helping the cooks in any way shape or form. Favorite nephew or not."

Keegan could hear her hoist her pants up higher on her belly and stifled a laugh. "Well, gee, *Aunt* Marg. You're putting me in a serious pickle."

"I'm not putting you in anything, young man. If you're so desperate for a macaroni and cheese recipe, why not visit your mother?"

Just the word was like a spur in Keegan's side. He and the woman who birthed him just didn't have that relationship. And even if they did, Victoria Flanagan was a worse cook than Keegan, if that were even possible. "Come on, you know my mom. She is too busy and too helpless."

"You can't be too busy and too helpless," Margaret-June replied.

"Well, if anyone can be busy and helpless at the same time, it's my mom."

"In that case, why not ask your lady friend?"

"Bo?"

"I always thought her name was Roberta. Roberta Delaney, right? Dick and Dorothy's oldest?"

"She goes by Bo and has since she was just a kid."

"How'd she get that nickname, anyway?"

Keegan closed his eyes and regretted ever calling sweet Aunt Marg. "She gave it to herself."

"She made up her own nickname?" Margaret-June started cackling again, and Keegan pressed the pad of his thumb into his eye sockets.

"Yes," he groaned, not embarrassed for Bo but rather frustrated with himself for letting the conversation get this far.

"You know what, Keegan?"

"What, Aunt Marg?"

"I think I might like this girl after all."

Chapter 9

Bo had just finished talking to the director for the Apache County Rodeo when her phone buzzed with a voicemail. It was Keegan.

She listened to the message with the glee of a schoolgirl. Keegan Flanagan was not a nervous person. And yet, after just a day of her aloofness, there he was, a bumbling wreck in her in-box.

Giddily, she dialed him back.

"It's you," he answered.

"It's me." Bo smiled to herself. Maybe Mary knew what she was talking about.

"Did you get my message?"

"Yes, the robbery. Is everyone okay?" Bo's voice dropped an octave, and she wondered if she'd have been better off seeing about the robbery instead of the rodeo.

"Yeah. No injuries. Have you gone down to the gas station yet? Talked to the clerk?"

"Oh, no, actually." Relaxing somewhat, she eased back into her chair.

"Oh."

A pause took hold of the phone line as they both awkwardly searched for the next thing to say.

"I will, though. I just have to cover this other piece first."

"What is the other piece about?"

Bo could hear Keegan growing impatient.

"The rodeo. I, uh, I'm covering some upcoming events on the mountain," she answered, now chewing at her thumbnail.

"I thought you were going for grit?" he replied.

"Yeah, well. I am. I just have to get these pieces done, too. You know how it is. Small-town rag and all that."

"Well, let me know if you have any questions about the break-in. I'll be around the station until five—unless I'm called out."

Bo grinned. "Do you have dinner plans?"

"Actually, that was the other reason I called you."

"Oh?" she pulled her hand away from her mouth and fiddled with the mouse pad on her laptop, navigating away from Dean Zick's social media profile. The rodeo director could wait. Her boyfriend had a dinner question.

"Bo, do you know of any good mac 'n' cheese recipes?"

IT WAS JUST BEFORE six as Bo grabbed her glass casserole dish from her back seat and hauled it up the deck to Keegan's front door.

Before she could so much as ring the bell, he appeared, smiling from ear to ear with a bottle of wine in one hand and a cooking mitt pinched in the other. "Your sous chef awaits you," he drawled.

Bo pecked him on the cheek and moved into Keegan's tidy kitchen—tidier than ever, she noted silently.

"All right, Ranger, did you secure the ingredients?" she asked, glancing down at his long oaken counter until her eyes fell upon two brown grocery sacks.

"Yes, ma'am," he whispered into her ear as he wrapped the wine-glass-wielding arm around her waist and pulled her in for a second kiss. Bo liked where this was going.

"No funny business, mister," she chided playfully evading a third and fourth kiss.

Keegan retreated to the kitchen table and poured them each a glass before plucking two, brand-new aprons from a hook on the side of the refrigerator and draping one over her head. Finally, he tied the thin strings in a tight knot at the small of her back before whipping her around and wrapping her in his arms.

Bo squirmed free, grabbed the other apron from Keegan and did the same, pulling it over his dark hair until it settled at the base of his neck before pushing his stolid waist in a circle and tying off the back.

He turned back to her and shook a finger. "No funny business, Chef," he admonished mockingly. Bo smirked and reached for her glass of wine, taking a small sip before she set about the business of pulling out the items from his interpretation of the shopping list.

"Generic noodles? That won't fly for the cook-off," she tsked.

Keegan blew out an exaggerated sigh and pushed a hand through his hair. "I told you I needed help."

"Next time, follow the list to the letter. It's the first step in any good recipe—gourmet *or* down home."

"Noted," he replied, swigging from his wineglass and cracking his knuckles as he passed her three bags of shredded cheese. "Sharp. Mild. Medium. Seems to me I could have gotten three bags of medium."

"Pre-shredded? Oh dear. You *do* have a lot to learn." Bo massaged her temples as though a headache formed, but she didn't admit that she, too, used bags of shredded cheese when she whipped up a dish of Mama's Mountain Mac, her mother's locally famous dish.

"I'll tell you what I have to learn, and it has *nothing* to do with shopping." Keegan set their wine glasses on the table and took her hands in his. Out of nowhere, it seemed, country music crawled across the ceiling and toward them. Keegan pulled Bo into a slow two-step across the hardwood floor. "I didn't know you were such a particular gal, Roberta Delaney," he whispered down into her ear.

Bo blinked up. "Really? I guess you're right, then."

"Right about what?"

"That you have a lot to learn about me."

They moved together a moment longer before Bo pushed away and insisted they get back to practicing the recipe. It felt a little too warm in the kitchen to let the cold ingredients sit much longer.

Chapter 10

Less than an hour later, Bo and Keegan were gobbling down their last bites of Mama's Mountain Mac as near-empty wine glasses kissed in the center of the table.

"Okay, okay," Keegan wiped his hands off on a paper towel and pressed a finger to the side of his head. "Cook the noodles al dente, drain, add a layer to the pan, layer in cheese mixture, repeat times three, add a splash of milk, a stick of butter—sliced and laid out across the top—salt and pepper, bake on 350 for 35 minutes or until golden and crispy on top."

"You got it," she answered, beaming proudly back at him. "If you don't win the cook-off, you'll have no one to blame but yourself. That right there is a winning recipe." Bo paused, wiping her own hands on a paper towel and looking around nervously. "There's only one thing…"

"What?" Keegan's voice turned panicky, and Bo broke out into a giggle.

"People might recognize it and call you a fraud!"

"Oh, please. No one will know it's your *mom's* recipe."

"For being a small-town boy, you sure don't seem to understand how small towns work, Ranger." She rose from the table and reached for his plate and fork, effectively clearing the table.

"Oh, sure I do. A week of the same old, same old, then something interesting happens, then four months of the same old, same old. And it just repeats itself."

Bo returned from the sink and sat next to Keegan with her back up against the table's edge. "Yeah. Tell me about it. So why do you love it so much?"

"I don't know," he answered honestly, his eyes looking past her and to his bed. The pillows sat almost squarely against the headboard. Beneath them, a blue quilt spread across the queen-sized mattress. Aunt Marg had made it for him years before. He cherished it and hesitated to even use the quilt. But Keegan was practical and hated not to use it. Also, change.

He felt Bo study him for a moment before she slapped her hands on top of her thighs and stood up. "I better go. It's getting late, and Mary probably wants to head home."

"You're still working the front desk, eh?"

"Well, yeah. Nothing has changed in the last forty-eight hours since I've seen you, believe it or not," she replied, her voice dipping lightly into sarcasm.

"Yeah," he answered, chuckling half-heartedly. "Do you enjoy living there? At the Lodge?"

Bo raised her eyebrows. "It's comfortable enough."

"Do you ever want your own place?" Keegan spread a hand around. But it wasn't an offer, and he dropped his hand sheepishly. "I mean, you don't mind living in a bed-and-breakfast?"

"I don't need a lot of space to be happy. Just like you, you know." She winked at him and Keegan felt his insides turn to mush. Where had these conversations been in the last several months?

THE RANGER'S MOUNTAIN BRIDE

"So you could stay there forever? Or...?" He was trying to get at something, though what he didn't know.

"No, of course not. It's one reason I've been thinking about moving, actually. Since you brought it up, you know..."

"You wouldn't live here?" There it was. The thing he was trying to get at. He licked his lips and waited for her answer.

"Keegan, I'm not playing house with you. We've been over this. You agree. And, besides, you are the one who wants nothing to change, right?"

Keegan stood and gripped her waist in his oversized hands. "Bo, you know me better than I know myself."

But somehow, it was the wrong thing to say. Because instead of offering to stay for their ritual hot cocoa by the fire, Bo came up with the lamest excuse he'd ever heard. "I'm going to a seminar tomorrow. *Ethics in Reporting* or something. Plus, I have to wrap up this rodeo piece tonight and send it in. I'd love to stay longer, Keegan, but I have to go."

And that wasn't even what surprised Keegan the most. Oh, no.

What surprised him the most was that she hadn't mentioned a single thing about the robbery.

After he walked her to her car and stood out in his drive as she rolled off into the night, Keegan absentmindedly began to chew on his thumbnail.

Chapter 11

THE RODEO RIDES IN ON THE SHOULDERS OF LOCAL FAMILY MAN

By Bo Delaney, *Mountain Times*

In this limited-time series of features, Reporter Bo Delaney will cover three Maplewood heroes, how they've impacted the community, and how the community has impacted them.

APACHE COUNTY—Just by looking at him, you know Dean Zick is a country man. Clad in Wrangler jeans (complete with a tobacco ring in the rear pocket) and standing tall in cowboy boots with a Stetson set neatly atop his head, Zick is the very image of a rodeo director.

Luckily for Maplewood, he's *our* rodeo director.

Each year in the spring, the Apache County Rodeo tumbles into town like a lassoing rough-rider, splaying across the county fairgrounds into an Olympic-style display of all things cowboy—or cow*girl*, as Zick is quick to correct.

THE RANGER'S MOUNTAIN BRIDE

Since 1995, Zick has been the man in charge of navigating everything from the line-up of competitions, to the coordination of food and drink vendors, all the way to the awards ceremony and removal of porta-Johns.

Oh, and don't mind the porta-John reference; Dean himself asked that I include that bit. After all, he says, "When it comes to an event of any size, creature comforts come first." Without prompting, he assures me, "We even opt for the washing station upgrade, complete with pump sinks, hand soap, and paper towels." The last part Dean adds with a wink before chuckling to himself.

What's striking about Dean Zick is not his hard exterior nor his position with the rodeo. No. Dean Zick stands out because he blends in.

With whom? You might ask. Well, with us. Dean is a born and bred mountain native, who came to be some years ago in the Zick family home out past Zick Ranch Road. A boy's boy who turned into a man's man and finally settled—like many Maplewood guys tend to—on making a family first, a home second, and a living third.

"Don't get me wrong," Dean admonishes, as he wags a dry-knuckled finger at me. "To have the first two, I had to make a living. Providing for my family puts a smile on my face and a beat in my heart."

When I ask Dean to share how he came to find success *and* happiness in his own rural community, he, again, chuckles beneath his trim mustache. "Well, Miss Delaney. I wasn't *looking* for it."

Learn more about Dean Zick and the Apache County Rodeo by visiting www.acrodeo.com.

Bo Delaney is an investigative reporter for the *Mountain Times*, covering local and late-breaking news around the mountain and in Maplewood.

Chapter 12

Keegan had just finished showering when he got the call. An all-points bulletin. Mayor Elect Martin Sherwood on the lam. No other information except local officials are alerted to be on the watch for Sherwood, now a fugitive from the law.

Without thinking, Keegan called Bo.

"Hey, everything all right?" her voice was low, indicating she was either climbing out of bed late or creeping into her office early. One never knew with that girl.

Keegan cleared his throat as he jumped in his truck and punched the key into the ignition. "Have you heard?"

"Heard what?" Now garbled, background noise over her voice gave away that she just woke up and likely overslept her alarm. "Keegan, what happened?"

"Martin Sherwood," he repeated, lamely, unsure what—exactly—to share. "There's a warrant out for his arrest."

"You're kidding. The *new mayor*?" Incredulity took the place of grogginess and Bo snapped to attention. "Why?"

He turned onto the highway and toward the station, unaware of what his role could be in the manhunt. "I don't have any more info. I'm heading into the station now for a debriefing and assignment. Bo," he went on, desperation tinting his words. "This isn't... part of our deal, okay?"

His knuckles turned white along the top of his steering wheel as he arrived at the station and hesitated just long enough to get Bo's word that she'd keep it quiet. For now, at least.

"What do you mean? I can't report anything? Keegan, if there's an APB out, then this story is fair game. It's been broadcasted by now. That's the whole point."

"I know, I know, but—" his promotion hung in the air above their phone call. Keegan needed things to be smooth. He needed the pay raise to add on to his cabin so he didn't have to bring Bo home to little more than a studio for dinners and hot cocoa. And, on top of everything, he needed no more personal involvement in the case than it would already seem he had.

"Is it because of your dad?" Bo asked, her tone softening.

"Well, it doesn't help that he was pushed out of office, but no. I just want to play it cool. Keep things clean, you know?" He rubbed the back of his neck and watched as a few other officers entered the building. "Bo, I have to go. Promise me you won't report?"

Her reply worried him. "Keegan, jeez. You're making me feel weird."

After blowing out a sigh, he found something to say. Something to get her off the line so he could get to work. "Why don't you just go work on that rodeo story. I'll call you when I can, all right?"

"Sure, all right. I have that regional training today, remember? So if I don't answer right away, text me. Please, Keegan?"

"Yeah, yeah. Gotta go. Bye, Bo."

WHY HE EVEN CALLED her at all was beyond Bo. Was it a sign that their relationship was taking a turn for the more serious? Did he need reassurance from her he could handle such an important case?

Was he desperate to get something off his chest that Bo couldn't quite put her finger on?

Unaware but dying for details, she drove to work. From there, she'd grab her press badge and laptop and head over to Lowell for the professional development.

The one good thing about being a reporter was that if she couldn't get the hot gossip from her family and friends, she would get it from her colleagues.

"Roberta, hi!" Annabelle Jackson was waving wildly at Bo from her spot at the front table.

Bo cringed on two accounts. One, she hated to sit in the front row. And two, she hated to be called her given name.

Still, Bo remembered her manners and so waved back at Annabelle before taking a seat near the back.

Three hours and one boring presenter later, the seminar had concluded. Bo had gained little insight but could at least add the hours to her resume. Just in case.

Throughout the session, Bo could not stop thinking about Keegan and the APB. He hadn't texted or called, and now she was desperate. So, she did the only thing there was to do: hover by the refreshments until Annabelle all but clawed her way over to Bo.

"Roberta! How are things at the *Times*?"

Bo shoved a stale bagel into her mouth and shrugged. "Same old, same old," she answered through chews. "And the *Gazette*?"

Annabelle and Bo weren't *so* different. "Great. But I'm itching to get out of here so I can chase this mayor story. My editor put someone else on it when he remembered I had signed up for this thing." She waved around her, irritation coloring her already rosy cheeks. "Bo, do *you* know anything?" Annabelle's voice dropped to a hiss and her eyes darted around the thinning group of county reporters.

"Yeah, I know. Keegan told me about it, and I'm-—" Bo drew her hand to her mouth quickly. She'd completely forgotten herself. She'd fallen into Annabelle's trap. Like a wild animal scavenging for a sinewy bone. Her heart dropped back in her chest and anxiety pounded in her head. Bo wadded up the last chunks of bagel into her paper towel and began to chew on her thumbnail as she avoided Annabelle's greedy gaze as she groped for a way to finish the sentence.

Annabelle beat her to the punch. "Keegan? Keegan *Flanagan*? He's the ranger who recovered those hikers, right? Is he a press liaison for the department, or..." The woman's meticulous eyebrows furrowed down beneath the horizon of her lashes and she inched toward Bo.

"No. Hey, I actually have an interview," Bo fibbed. "I'm covering another story. The news doesn't sleep, you know."

"What could be hotter than this mayor scandal?" Annabelle pried.

Bo searched for an honest answer, thoughts about Keegan clouding her ability to think straight. His mother came to mind, and something she'd seen recently on social media. "It's a

THE RANGER'S MOUNTAIN BRIDE 63

luncheon I'm prepping for. A big deal actually. The Mountain Realtors' Association is hosting a luncheon, and I'm doing an expose on the keynote speaker."

And just like that, Bo realized it could be true.

She could interview her own boyfriend's mother. For Mary's challenge.

The only problem was, she'd be crazy to let the mayor story slip through her fingers. That sort of a piece could launch her from tiny Maplewood into a bigger publication. Heck, she could skip right past *Tucson* and maybe land a gig with Phoenix. Maybe in Phoenix men wouldn't be so hesitant about marriage and editors would be willing to give small-town reporters a shot.

Maybe Bo wouldn't even have a say in the matter... if her career came knocking, would she really let a commitment-shy boyfriend hold her back?

Her professional life had suddenly turned into a very distinct fork in the road.

Mary's silly challenge sat at the end of one road—like a pretty pink package—promising nothing more than the fulfillment of a promise to her sister.

Mayor-Elect Sherwood, local renegade and modern-day outlaw (though why, she didn't know) sat at the other end—like a plump prize pig—promising a juicy story to satiate Bo's interest in the world around *her and* a promotion to work more stories just like that one.

But deep inside, Bo couldn't let *anyone* down. Not Mary. Not Keegan. And not the news-reading public.

Chapter 13

Keegan oversaw local search efforts on the Sherwood case. They had yet to set up a press release, and he knew Bo was probably clamoring for all the information she could get. But it wasn't time yet. There were a million things to handle, least of all how the newspapers would spin the story.

He'd been working all morning to coordinate dynamic and systematic search efforts within the town limits and all the way to the county lines. He was slated to make the rounds to Sherwood family homes for interviews, but first he needed to take five.

A good law enforcement officer knew when to push and when to rein it in. With roadblocks stationed appropriately, he felt secure in using the restroom and grabbing a coffee before heading out.

As he went to the break room, he checked his phone. Sure enough, a text from Bo. He wished he could give her something—anything. But he couldn't. Still, his heart swelled a bit when he read her message.

Thinking of you. Stay safe out there. I have another story to follow while I wait for your update. No rush. Love you, Keegan.

Love.

Now that was a word. One they hadn't used often together. In fact, they hadn't used it in a while. Keegan felt guilt tug at his chest as he put together a good-enough response.

Waiting for the next round of updates to schedule press release. Boss says no tips until then. Hope to lock this down soon and sweep you back to my place for hot cocoa. I'd like to talk about things.

He hit send before composing a second message.

Love you too, Bo.

But that was how he felt *before* the phone call came into his office.

"Flanagan—press call on line one," Sally hollered to him as he appeared from the only restroom break he'd taken all morning.

Assuming it was Bo putting on an act, he answered the call flirtatiously, adding subtle innuendo he'd hope she'd read into. "Nothing's locked down yet, but I'm hoping we can make that happen soon," he drawled lazily as he eased into his desk chair for a quick reprieve before returning to check on the choppers who'd been assigned to the northeastern segment.

"Well, I like the sound of that." It wasn't Bo. No. The nasally voice on the other end of the line was entirely unfamiliar and exactly what cops thought of when they thought of meddling journalists.

He cleared his throat. "Pardon me, who's speaking?"

"Annabelle Jackson with the *Lowell Gazette*. Howdy, Ranger Flanagan. I have just a couple questions about the current situation with Mayor-Elect Sherwood if you don't mind—"

"The *Lowell Gazette*?" he cut her off, standing and pressing a hand down onto his desk as blood throbbed in his temples.

"Right, sir. We're the circulation out of Lowell, Arizona. Just a twenty-minute drive southwest of Maplewood—"

Again, Keegan interrupted the woman. "I know where Lowell is, and I *know* what the *Gazette* is. The Sheriff's Office is not answering any press questions right now. You can expect a release in a couple hours. Have a good day." He began to hang up the receiver, but Annabelle chimed in with one more question.

"Then, with all due respect, Ranger, how come your reporter girlfriend is talking about it?"

Keegan frowned, confused. "I don't know what you're talking about, ma'am."

"Roberta Delaney. She was clearly apprised of the situation early this morning. I saw her at a seminar and she told me all about it."

Chapter 14

Bo felt terrible about opening her mouth to Annabelle. But not that terrible. After all, she didn't say much. What could Annabelle possibly write about the case? Nothing. If the smarmy Lowell reporter learned anything about the Sherwood case, it would have to come from someone other than Keegan Flanagan's girlfriend.

Still, that Bo had said anything at all put her in a bit of a pickle. Now, she'd have to play dumb until the press conference. She wouldn't be able to ambulance chase any cop cars or listen in on the scanner at the office.

So, to kill the time she set about tracking down someone who had nothing to do with the Maplewood scandal. The interviewee for Bo's next human interest piece.

Mary would be happy to see Bo moving nicely through the challenge, and Bo's boss, Mr. Ketchum, would be happy to have a fresh story. The Dean Zick piece was a hit. Rumor had it, Mr. Ketchum had even sent the story to his brother in the valley—a man who ran the parent company of the *Times*, Ketchum Print and Press.

That was likely just a rumor to pad Bo's ego. Mr. Ketchum probably didn't send it. And his brother probably wouldn't care if he did.

Pulling up to the Mountain Realty office was a bit nerve-wracking. Bo knew Keegan's parents, but only in so much as she knew *anyone* in Maplewood. She didn't know them in her role as his significant other. Nor did they know her as Keegan's girlfriend. She wondered if they *knew* she was Keegan's girlfriend.

And that caused Bo to wonder if she was even Keegan's girlfriend to begin with.

Then she remembered the text burning a hole in her satchel.

Hope to lock this down soon and sweep you back to my place for hot cocoa. I'd like to talk about things.

Love you too, Bo.

They were more than boyfriend and girlfriend. And Bo had a very good feeling that any plans she ever had to leave Maplewood would begin and end with this whole challenge Mary had put her up to. Playing hard to get was obviously the best choice. Because Keegan seemed to feed off her absence.

And, anyway, Bo sort of liked the human interest pieces. Maybe more so than the dangerous news stories. There was an honesty and safety, a comfort and familiarity in writing the stories of the people who'd made up the fabric of her very home.

She stepped boldly up the three glazed steps and onto a monogrammed doormat outside a massive, knotty wood door complete with a heavy iron knocker. Knocking twice, Bo tucked her satchel neatly along her side and lifted her chin as her mother had told her to. No nail biting. No faltering.

This was a woman-to-woman meeting of the minds.

And, if Bo was lucky, a meeting of the hearts, too.

THE RANGER'S MOUNTAIN BRIDE 69

"Roberta?" Victoria Flanagan was every inch the woman Bo expected her to be and then some. With Keegan's angular bone structure and the refinement of a lady not raised in a small-town, she filled the door frame with grace and superiority. "Roberta *Delaney*?"

Bo regretted everything in that moment. Stumbling across the advertisement for the luncheon. Being a lowly reporter. Coming from a family of six. Growing up on a farm. Dating this woman's *son*...

Then her good sense kicked in.

"Hello, Mrs. Flanagan. You can call me Bo. I'm here from the *Mountain Times*. We're covering your luncheon tomorrow. I'd love to interview you ahead of the event. Mind if I come in?"

A brisk walk later, Bo was sitting in a spacious corner office decorated in what she could only describe as mountain chic. Two windows spread across adjacent walls behind Victoria. Through one, her visitors had a view of a lavish garden. Through the other, the national forest. Vast hiding space for someone like Sherwood. Bo wondered how Keegan was. If he was stressed. If he ever worried about his parents or his mother. Or even her.

"This won't take long," Bo began, flipping open her trusty notebook as she pointed the eraser-end of her pencil toward the windows. "Great view. Shame you face opposite," Bo said then took a swig from the water bottle Victoria had offered.

The woman didn't glance behind her. "Everyone points that out, but the view isn't for me. It's for my customers. I like to show them what *could* be theirs. This mountain of ours has so much to offer. I know you agree, dear."

Bo nodded. "Mrs. Flanagan, can you tell me a little about what brought you to the mountain originally? Why you chose Maplewood to throw down roots and raise your family?"

Leaning back into her ergonomically therapeutic chair, Victoria sucked in a deep breath. "Well, I didn't choose Maplewood. Maplewood chose me, you know."

Bo glanced up and raised her eyebrows, nodding the woman on interestedly.

"I met Bobby—my husband—in college at ASU. The business school. It was love at first sight, really, but he was dead set on returning to Maplewood to take care of his own ailing parents. I was a girl in love."

Bo felt Victoria's stare but nodded. "I see. And what did you think of Maplewood back then? That would have been the—ah—seventies? Eighties?"

Victoria smiled tightly. "Around then, yes. Maplewood hasn't changed all that much. Same small town. Same locals, you know. New tourists, however. In fact, over the last eight years, we've steadily grown our summer residency by two percent each year—give or take. This past summer was especially fruitful. The good snowfall really helped remind the valley people what we have to offer. I sold 15 homes alone between April and October. It's a personal record and may well be a regional record, too. All second-home owners of course, which is great for Maplewood. The more people we can bring up here, even just part time, the better we can be."

Inexplicably, Bo felt herself gag. She pushed the sensation down her throat and lifted her eyes to Victoria, studying Keegan's mother momentarily. It made no sense, really. How could *Keegan* have been raised by this woman? He was so much the opposite. A champion of locals. A do-it-yourselfer. Was Bob Flanagan so great that he off-set any damage by Victoria? Or was it that Victoria was so consumed by other parts of her life, that her parenting was irrelevant?

"Can you tell me a little about your family? A big part of this segment is a personal touch. Perhaps you read the piece on Dean Zick?"

"Hm, all right. What can I tell you that you don't know?" She shifted uncomfortably, uncrossing and re-crossing her leg.

"Your husband and children. Family life. We attract a readership who values that," Bo reminded her with a pointed look and a smile.

"Ah, well gosh. Bob does Bob. He's always trying to be involved in the community somehow. Help people. He's almost never home—or maybe that's me." A sharp cackle startled Bo from her notes but she forced herself to concentrate as Victoria went on. "It's true, dear. I'm a small-town workaholic. What a contradiction, huh? But, Roberta, I'm passionate. I'm passionate about bringing mountain home ownership to those who love to visit."

"And Keegan and his brothers?" Bo pressed.

"They practically raised themselves—" She stopped mid-sentence and stared daggers at Bo. "Let me rephrase, please. Bob and the boys were so close growing up. Hunting and building. They were all such boys' boys." She paused, looking thoughtful. "And now, really men's men." A twinkle nearly caught her, but she shook it away. "You can quote that."

Bo smiled sweetly and asked the next question. "What are you most proud of in your role as one of Maplewood's community leaders?"

Victoria didn't hesitate. "Setting an example."

Confused, Bo asked for clarification.

"Well, Roberta. I never wanted to live here—don't quote that. But I made a home of it. I found my place here and, well, thrived." She flashed white teeth at Bo. "And now, Roberta, I love it. I really do."

For the first moment in their conversation, sincerity colored the woman's voice. Bo glanced out the windows behind her and thought of something else to ask. She needed one more thing. "Mrs. Flanagan?" she asked, almost meek.

"Yes, dear?"

"What do you see for Maplewood? I mean the future of it? And your family, too—their place here?"

"Despite it all, I hope my family carries on my legacy here."

Bo smiled and set her pencil on her notebook. "And how would you define your legacy, Mrs. Flanagan?"

"I hope at least one of my children raises his family here and makes a beautiful home."

Bo was caught off guard. The whole interview was moving in the exact opposite direction. But through it all, Bo couldn't help but relate to the woman—on some level at least.

After Victoria had walked Bo to the front door and thanked her for such a nice meeting, Bo did something that felt foreign to both women. But it was necessary. She opened her arms to hug Victoria. The woman, unfazed, responded in kind, adding an air kiss to each of Bo's cheeks.

"Mrs. Flanagan, you can call me Bo. Everyone does," she said before stepping through the door.

"And you can call me Victoria." She smiled back at Bo and leaned into one hip, measuring Bo for a moment.

It was time to leave. Past time, really. But Bo had one more thing to say. "Victoria, by the way, I'm dating Keegan."

Victoria returned an impish grin then winked at her. "Yes, I know, Bo. He adores you."

LOCAL REALTOR IS MORE THAN JUST A TRANSPLANT

By Bo Delaney, *Mountain Times*

In this limited-time series of features, Reporter Bo Delaney will cover three Maplewood heroes, how they've impacted the community, and how the community has impacted them.

MAPLEWOOD—Tenacious. If one word would describe Mountain Realty President and Owner it would be *tenacious*.

Victoria Flanagan never set out to be, as her husband of 38 years calls her, a "mountain mama." But, that's exactly what Victoria is. After meeting Robert during her undergraduate degree at ASU, Victoria hesitated to follow him to his hometown of Maplewood.

After all, Victoria was born and raised in the big city and always planned on establishing herself among the titans of the Phoenix real estate industry.

"But," Victoria says as she stares down at her antique, princess-cut engagement ring, which rides high above a sturdier looking yellow gold band, "I watered the grass here." She glances up and waves a bejeweled hand around the room. "Oh," she adds, catching me as I admire her jewelry. "Family heirlooms. Almost all of it. People don't know that about me."

What she means is that there's more than meets the eye. Though primped and bedazzled and easily mistaken for a former movie star's wife, rather than the former mayor's wife, Victoria is the real deal. Eschewing the tacky for the authentic, she appears—at first—to be a contradiction.

After moving to the mountain with her new husband in the early eighties, Victoria made small-town life as glamorous as she could—saving every penny and putting it toward renovating the Flanagan family cabin into one of the most beautiful lodges in Maplewood.

"I was lucky," Victoria says, sighing happily as she passes a framed photograph of her family for my inspection. "Bob supported every dream I ever had. He knew the value of compromise. When I agreed to move here, he let me call the rest of the shots. The early days were lean, while I worked as the manager for a cabin rental company. But we made it out."

Smiling proudly, Victoria admits she sometimes wishes her two younger sons would have stayed or returned to Maplewood to grow their own families. "But I understand the need to find one's way. And anyway," she goes on. "I have my eldest son, Keegan here. He didn't exactly get to live a life of luxury like his younger brothers. Now that everyone is grown up and Danny and Billy have their own lives elsewhere, I have an opportunity to spoil him a little."

When asked what she means, she looks thoughtfully out the window. "Keegan is a true Maplewood man. He takes after his father. He works hard and never stops." Glancing briefly at me, a small smile shapes Victoria's immaculately painted lips. "I just hope he finds time to enjoy life up here, too. That's the one thing I have to remind myself of quite often. Maplewood has everything to offer. If only the locals would play tourist once in a while."

For details on tomorrow's Realtor's Association Luncheon or if you are interested in touring mountain homes for sale, call Victoria Flanagan at 555.297.1599.

Bo Delaney is an investigative reporter for the *Mountain Times*, covering local and late-breaking news around the mountain and in Maplewood.

Chapter 15

"I can't believe you," Keegan hissed as he stepped away from the podium and took Bo by the elbow off the stage and over to the grassy knoll where every reporter in the county would soon stand and wait for their update.

Bewildered, Bo whipped her head behind her, searching for some cause of his sudden anger. "What are you talking about?" she hissed back.

Now assured they were far enough from the officers who were setting up, Keegan dipped his head and answered, "Annabelle Jackson. She called me this morning and said you'd told her everything."

Bo leaned away, disgust twisting her features. "*Everything*? I didn't know *anything*. How could I tell her *everything*?"

Keegan frowned deeper. "That's what she said. Anyway, you weren't supposed to say a thing. Bo, I could get in deep trouble if people think I'm sharing confidential information to the press before I'm allowed. Our deal was that I'd help you within the bounds of ethics. But if anyone knew about it, it sure as heck would not look very ethical that I'm ranting to my girlfriend who blabs to any reporter who'll listen."

Shaking her head, Bo glared back. "I'm sorry, but it was an accident. All I said was that I heard about the case."

"You didn't mention my name?"

THE RANGER'S MOUNTAIN BRIDE 77

Bo paused and looked beyond him for a moment before returning her gaze. "I don't remember. But I had nothing to tell her, so it doesn't matter. I swear Keegan, come on." Her voice turned to a plea, but he had no idea how to answer.

The Sherwood story was heating up, and he was due to oversee the press release. Would Annabelle be there? Would things settle? He couldn't be sure.

"Fine, whatever. Just, promise me to keep things above board, okay?"

Bo nodded. "I haven't even been covering the story, Keegan. I'm sorry about the Annabelle thing, but I promise it won't go anywhere."

Trusting her, he offered a quick peck on the cheek before returning to the podium area just in time for the chief to come out and run a microphone test.

Soon enough, vans rolled up to the curb and reporters with their cameramen at their heels waded through the thick grass to stand expectant before the chief.

Keegan kept his eye on Bo, who sort of dawdled on the edge, alone and quiet. He felt bad for getting on her case, but he couldn't risk the promotion. It meant everything to him. To *them*. She just didn't know it.

Minutes later, a sedan parked at the end of the line of news vans and out stepped Annabelle, her hair like a helmet and a chunky recorder in her hand. She stomped up to the knoll, her eyes searching.

Keegan caught her gaze and, for a minute, he could have sworn she smirked at him.

But it was too hard to tell, and the chief began reviewing what they'd learned so far.

That Keegan and his team had found Mayor-Elect Sherwood.

WITH THE PRESS RELEASE over, Bo watched Annabelle, unnerved by the woman's mere presence. It turned out she was right to be unnerved, because once the vans had dribbled away, off to put together compelling reports on the news that Sherwood was stealing Apache County Rodeo funds to the sum of over forty thousand dollars.

To Bo, the story could be a game changer. She knew just how to spin it—victimizing the small town and heralding the sheriff's office, particularly Keegan.

But then Annabelle appeared, in the center of the grassy knoll, staring at Bo while the officers began to pack up their equipment and move back inside. Bo searched for Keegan, catching his eyes dart from Annabelle to her. It was like some twisted love triangle. But there was no love for Annabelle. That much was clear.

"This is an important story," Annabelle called across the grass to Keegan. Bo walked faster, her heart pounding in her chest, while she chewed on her thumbnail.

"I couldn't agree more," Keegan answered, his face expressionless.

Bo intervened. "Yep, sure is. Time to go write about it, right, Annabelle?"

"Actually, I'm talking about you two," Annabelle snarled sweetly.

Bo stole a nervous glance at Keegan then pressed the woman for more. "What do you mean?"

"It's inappropriate for a law enforcement official to share information with a member of the press. I doubt your supervisor would like to hear that you're... courting Ms. Delaney, so to speak..."

Aghast, Bo opened her mouth to speak, but she felt Keegan's hand on her shoulder. He had moved behind her but now pulled her back slightly, protecting her from Annabelle.

"I'm well within my rights and privileges to share with my significant other when I have to report for an emergency. There is no scandal here, if that's what you're looking for, Miss..." Keegan scratched his temple. "I'm sorry; can you remind me of your name?"

"Annabelle Jackson," she answered lamely. "Then I suppose it's also appropriate for Roberta, in her official capacity as a member of the press, to share early details of the case ahead of the press release?"

"You're trying to start trouble where there is none. Listen, Ms. Jackson, this case is no longer a mystery. You've got all the details you need. If you were disappointed the manhunt had ended, well, I'm sorry to hear that your first concern is a salacious story rather than a happy ending."

Annabelle pouted. "I'm thrilled to hear you and your team, Ranger, have apprehended Sherwood. I take issue with Roberta's early access to the case."

"I didn't write anything, did I? And what did you learn from me, exactly, Annabelle?" It was a petulant question, but Bo couldn't help herself.

The woman took a step backward. "I find it to be exceptional that you two date and *you*"—she lifted a manicured fingernail and pointed it firmly at Bo—"write it up."

"If it's a story you want, Annabelle, it's a story you can have. The Sherwood case is yours. I'm not interested."

Keegan turned and glared meaningfully at Bo. Annabelle cocked her head. "What?" she asked.

"I have bigger fish to fry. I'm running a limited series of exposés, and it's my focus right now. Sherwood is yours." Bo let out a sigh and realized that, though the Sherwood story would net her serious professional credit, all that she said was true. Interviewing the locals had turned into her preference. Passion, even. Sherwood was a Phoenix transplant and irrelevant to the fabric of Maplewood. Her *home*.

"Bo, you don't have to give up the story. You can both write a piece," Keegan reasoned.

She shook her head. "No, Annabelle wants the scoop. She is gunning for something big. She can have it." Bo paused and looked from the other reporter then up to Keegan. "I already have what I want."

Chapter 16

"She posted it!" Bo called from behind her laptop in his armchair by the fire. The temperatures dipped low that evening, and so it was only logical for the two of them to end the night with hot cocoa by the fire, as usual.

Keegan stirred powder into their mugs and crossed his cabin in long strides before setting the mugs on their proper coasters and standing beside Bo's chair to read her computer screen from over her shoulder.

MAPLEWOOD MAYOR-ELECT SHERWOOD EMBEZZLES RODEO FUNDS

By Annabelle Jackson, *Lowell Gazette*

MAPLEWOOD—In near-record time, the Apache County Sheriff's Office has apprehended and arrested would-be politician Martin Sherwood and charged him with embezzlement.

The question of a mishandling of funds became clear as Apache County Rodeo Director Dean Zick underwent a regularly scheduled audit.

Suspicious of foul play and uncomfortable with Sherwood's desire to be a close sponsor for the local event, he hit the alarm and brought his concerns and the audit findings to local law enforcement.

During an attempt to contact Sherwood at his home, law enforcement agents found stacks of cash and what appeared to be a getaway bag in plain sight, allowing them entry. Sherwood was nowhere to be seen, and his family and friends were concerned for his personal safety.

As locals by now know, a hot pursuit fell underway. It didn't last long. Ranger Keegan Flanagan and his team of search and rescue agents discovered Sherwood holed up in a restaurant in the Maplewood Ski Lodge.

Sherwood is now in custody at the Apache County Jailhouse. Questions can be directed to the sheriff's office. Stay tuned for exclusive updates with the *Gazette*.

Annabelle Jackson is a pavement-pounding investigative reporter for the Lowell Gazette, *the mountain's premier news source. She can be contacted on social media or by searching #annabelle.d.jackson.*

"What a cheese ball," Keegan muttered before crossing to his chair and settling in.

"Well, at least she's *Lowell's* cheese ball," Bo agreed, smiling as she reached for her mug and sipped carefully at it. "I'm happy for her. She wanted that boring story."

"Boring? We had a full-blown manhunt underway. What's with you lately, *Roberta*?" he teased, eyeing her over his steaming cocoa.

Bo returned her mug and stood, walking her laptop to his bed where she set it, closed. "I like adventure. Not political drama. And anyway, I wasn't lying," she continued, heading toward the restroom. "This human interest series... it's hooked me. I learned a lot today, actually."

Keegan tended to the fire before Bo returned, and together they squeezed into the armchair nearer the hearth, Bo's legs draped over his lap.

"What did you learn today?" he asked, tucking a strand of her dark hair behind her ear.

She grinned back at him, tilted her chin toward his hand and allowing him to tickle the side of her face before ducking his mouth to hers. Their lips brushed, momentarily, before she pulled back, biting down on her lower lip and closing her eyes.

"I interviewed your mom today," she admitted, squeezing her eyes shut harder and then peeking up out of one. Her blue iris glowed at him, and he shook his head.

"My *mom*?" he asked, confused. "Why?"

"For the human interest series. Mavens of Maplewood. That's what we decided to call it. I needed a big name, and I wanted a woman. And, I mean, she's my boyfriend's *mom*. Anyway..." she waved her hand in front of her. "I didn't know you had told her we were dating."

"Of course I told her. Both my parents know. Danny and Billy, too."

Bo made a face.

"What's wrong with that?" Keegan asked, defensive. Most people weren't fans of his younger brothers. In fact, years ago—before the two knuckleheads moved off the mountain and away for good—they had garnered a reputation in Maplewood. For being jerks, actually. Keegan agreed with the public, but he still talked to them from time to time. Both Danny and Billy had been excited to hear about Keegan's relationship with Bo.

Anyone would be excited for him. Bo was a catch. Keegan knew this.

"I just...I haven't been sure how serious we are," she answered, at last, swallowing and avoiding his gaze.

"We're serious. I mean... I am," he answered. "Bo, we're exclusive, right?"

Her eyes grew wide. "*I* am exclusively dating *you*," she replied, her hand pressed to her chest as though she'd been scandalized.

"Well, *I'm* exclusively dating *you*, too," he mimicked, cracking a smile and roping his arm around her waist, pulling her closer to him in the already-tight space. "Bo, I don't know if we've *said* it, but I know we've written it," he began, studying her.

"Written what?" she asked in return.

"Well, I love you, Bo. Like, a lot. As much as a man can love a woman, you know."

She beamed and tucked her chin down before looking up through her eyelashes at him. It was out of character. Bo wasn't a bat-your-eyelashes type of gal. But this coy mistress bit allured him.

"I love you, too, Keegan. As much as a woman can love a man." Her jaw leveled out and her smile faded somewhat, but she kept quiet for a moment.

"So, you're sticking around town, then. No plans to move? You're happy? How things are?" Keegan planned to offer her more. He did. But when he'd returned inside after the press conference—once Annabelle Jackson had been sufficiently de-escalated—his boss gave him a slap on the back and little else. The promotion he'd hoped to nab seemed further away than ever. And if Keegan would make a home for Bo, he needed that promotion. He refused to ask his parents for help.

The thought reminded him to ask something. Before she could answer his slew of questions, he added one more. "My mom didn't scare you off, did she? She can... my mom is an intense person. I guess you two are similar in some ways. Focused on your career. Anyway, I'm rambling here, Bo. Throw me a bone, something, anything." He pinned her with a serious stare and licked his lips.

"I'm happier than I've ever been, actually. I see what you mean about your mom. I think I learned a lot about you from her. She's intense. But, I know she loves you."

Keegan nodded, unsure she'd answered his questions.

Bo went on. "And, Keegan. She loves your dad, too. You know?"

He cocked his head, surprised by what felt like something of a judgment. An overstepping. A measurement against his family's dynamics. He blinked. "What do you mean?"

Immediately, she backtracked. "Nothing, nothing. I just... I'm sorry. That came out weird. I just... I think I have you figured out one minute, then everything changes. But when I met your mom—she's lovely, really Keegan—I felt like things became clearer for me."

He scratched his jaw and struggled to provide an answer.

Still, Bo kept talking. "I see why you keep tight control of your life. I see why you love your job. And, I see why you're hesitant about..." her sentence fell away, and she stared off to the rest of his cabin. "I see why you want to keep things just the way they are, I suppose."

She shut down. He wasn't sure where she was going, but he had an idea. "Bo, I know this place isn't much. But I have big plans. I want you to live here, eventually. When you're ready. I'll add on. It'll be more than a bachelor pad. I promise."

Bo shook her head. "You don't need to do any of that."

"But I am. I will. I'll do whatever it takes," he answered, searching her eyes.

She held a finger to his lips and leaned in. "You don't have to do a single thing, Keegan Flanagan. I love you just the way you are. I love your home. And I'm staying in Maplewood. But I can't move in."

Though he was still confused, they kissed. A deep, urgent kiss on Bo's end. A bewildered, empty kiss on his.

"So you won't move in?" he asked as they parted, at last.

Sadly, Bo stood. "Not yet," she answered. "We're not playing house, remember?"

And after squeezing his fingers in her hand, she gave him a final peck on the forehead before leaving. Back to the lodge. Further away from him than she'd ever seemed to be.

Chapter 17

"I left my computer at your place again. I need it for work. Should I swing by?" It was the Thursday before the cook-off, and Bo hadn't so much as chosen her subject for the expose, much less researched the event.

She and Keegan had gone back and forth with date nights—alternating between the lodge and his cabin. This was the second time now that she'd left her laptop on his bed. A psychologist might have something to say about the matter, but Keegan enjoyed any excuse to see her these days.

That much had become clear.

Between bites of his morning bagel, he answered, "Actually I can drop it off. I'm heading to the grocery store this morning to get ingredients for the cook-off. Kind of nervous."

"Exciting," she replied. And it was. They'd practiced the dish a second time, but he wasn't pushing his luck. Third time would hopefully be a charm at the event itself. "If you win, you have to dedicate your trophy to me. Do the winners get trophies?" she asked, packing her satchel in her room before she was slated to be downstairs to help serve breakfast alongside Mary.

"Isn't it your job to find out? You're writing about the whole thing, right?" he joked. "Hey, by the way, Bo. I need the recipe. Like, written down. Ingredients again, all that."

"You have it in your phone. I texted it to you two weeks ago."

"Yeah, but that's when I got all generic stuff. I want the real deal this time."

"Oh, wait!" She snapped her fingers, a lucky thought occurring to her. "I have it saved in a file on my laptop. You can pull it up and take a picture of it or whatever."

"Are you sure?" he pressed, now sitting in his car with her laptop sitting on his front seat.

"Of course. Just search for Mama's Mountain Mac. It'll come right up."

"Okay, I'll get a picture and drive over to the lodge. Love you, Bo."

"Love you, Keegan. See ya soon."

After he hung up and opened her laptop, he realized it had never shut down from the evening prior. Instead, it was asleep. As soon as the device glowed to life, Keegan was presented with Bo's email in-box.

A neat stack of opened messages sat in a row as he tried to navigate on the mouse pad toward the search box at the lower left-hand side of the screen.

Just as he began to type in *Mama*, a new message dinged its way into her in-box and flashed across the screen.

Keegan had no way of *not* seeing. It was there, in his face, clear as day.

From a man with a complicated email address. The subject and a preview of the message glared at him, and he read it before even realizing that he was reading at all.

Wow!

Bo, Would LOVE to meet. My number is...

Keegan felt sick.

Physically ill. The name seemed familiar, which doubled his nausea. Surely there had to be an explanation. He should never have opened her computer. Regret at reading the words clouded his judgment, and he refused to open the message to read on. It was a true Pandora's box, but learning anything else might just kill him.

It took every ounce of strength he could muster not to chuck the stupid computer out his window.

He had to talk to Bo.

Now.

Chapter 18

"*Chuck* Ketchum?" she repeated his words as they stood on the front deck of the Wood Smoke Lodge.

A line of sweat glistened along Keegan's brow, and fear lifted his chest in heaves. "Yeah," he spat, anger shading his voice.

"*Ketchum?*" she repeated, thoroughly confused.

"Yes, *Chuck Ketchum*. Don't you get email on your phone? Surely you've seen this jerk's message."

She could tell he hated to explain himself, and all she wanted to do was wrap him in a hug and tell him to calm down. But he was beside himself with rage—and it was all directed at *her*.

"Listen, Keegan," she replied, glancing behind her to determine that they were alone and no guests had wandered downstairs yet. "*Greg* Ketchum is my boss. The editor-in-chief at the *Times*. *Chuck* Ketchum... I have no clue. What does the email say?"

"*You* tell *me*, Bo," he replied, his voice softening only just.

"*You're* the one who was reading my email," she accused, now closing the door behind her, grabbing his arm, and dragging him to a set of Adirondack chairs that sat at the far end of the deck.

"It popped up on your computer. I didn't read the whole thing. I just saw the subject and the first few words. *Wow. Would LOVE to meet*," he quoted, his jaw set.

THE RANGER'S MOUNTAIN BRIDE 91

She racked her brain momentarily before it hit her. "Oh, I know who it is!" she declared, smiling now. "Mr. Ketchum's *brother*! The Phoenix guy!"

Keegan shrank into his seat. "*Who?*"

"Keegan, Mr. Ketchum sent my first expose to his brother who runs a printing press in Phoenix. He was proud of it and sent the guy a paper. I know, it's dumb. It was a short piece and didn't reveal much. But it had heart, Mr. Ketchum said."

"Heart? Huh? Whoa, whoa. Back up. Why did he email you, then?" Keegan asked. A fair question.

Bo didn't quite know. "I have an email app on my phone. I just haven't checked it. Let's see," she muttered, digging into her pocket and retrieving her device before navigating to her apps and opening the unread message.

Wow!

Bo,

Would LOVE to meet. My number is 555.542.9136. My brother sent me your piece on Dean Zick. He and I go way back to our bull-riding days in Tucson!! If you're ever looking for a job in the valley, call me. And if you talk to Dean again, please give him my regards.

Hope to read more of your work! Really great!

Your new friend in the biz,

Chuck

"Sounds kind of slimy, actually," Bo commented, clicking out of the message and setting her phone on the arm of the chair. "I can see why you got so mad, but—"

She didn't have to go on. Keegan rubbed his hands over his face before offering a sheepish half-grin. "Sorry, Bo. I really jumped to conclusions there."

"Yeah, you did," she replied, crossing her arms over her chest. "Can I have my computer back?"

He nodded and jogged out to his truck, returning shortly with the laptop. "I'll make it up to you somehow. I promise," Keegan offered, his eyes pleading somewhat.

Enjoying the attention, Bo grinned. "In that case, I need you to connect me with the director of the Ranger's Roundup."

"Huh?" he answered, scratching the back of his head.

"Word has it you know the director."

He stopped scratching his head. "Where did you hear that?"

"I called the sheriff's office just before you got here. They redirected me to you," she replied.

"Well, yeah. It's my dad's sister. Aunt Marg. Margaret-June Flanagan. That's her full name."

"Mind if I name drop you?" Bo asked, coy now.

"By all means. She'd be happy to meet you," he replied.

"You know," Bo began, tapping a finger on her lower lip. "It might make things easier if, instead of sending me blindly to your relative's house, you escorted me there. I mean it's related to your job, right? And she's your aunt, so..."

Keegan blew out a sigh. "She's a little... quirky, my aunt," he said, at last.

"I like quirky."

"Kinda overbearing, too," Keegan continued.

Bo studied him. "She won't like me?" It was a reasonable guess, and Keegan's face gave her the answer she needed. Bo gave Keegan a curt nod. "Right. Well, I'll change her mind. Don't worry."

She began to turn to head inside, but Keegan stood and grabbed her arm, whipping her around to face him. "Hey, now. I said I owed you. And I do. I'll take you over there, but you can't hold my aunt against me, okay? She's single and a little reclusive. She has high ideals of what I do with my life. I mean, she gave up on Billy and Danny. I'm the only nephew she has left to torture. Okay?"

"Keegan," Bo began to answer. "This is just a preliminary write-up. Info for the town on the event. I'm not even going to interview her for a feature like the others."

"Oh," he answered, sounding wounded. "Well, okay, then."

"But, Keegan," she went on. He glanced back up at her, in time for Bo to reach up to his face and hold his jaw in her hand. "I'm an investigative journalist. If she has something I want to know, then you can bet I'll get it out of her."

Chapter 19

ANNUAL RANGER ROUND-UP GETS A THEME

By Bo Delaney, *Mountain Times*

MAPLEWOOD—The Apache County Sheriff's Office is known around the state for two things: their dedication to upholding the law *and* their yearly cook-off event. People come from every corner of Arizona to sample the goods that the mountain law enforcement team has to offer.

As some may recall, last year's dish was chili. Ranger Dan Thompson stole the show with his mother's spicy take on a down-home favorite, complete with jalapeno cornbread and honey butter. Though all the entries were enough to fill a party-goer's belly, Dan and his mom proved that Arizona chili doesn't have to be boring.

Lately, rumors have been swirling about what our trusty sheriff's office will be asked to cook up. Some have wondered about brick-fired pizza. Some think

THE RANGER'S MOUNTAIN BRIDE

a burger fest. Many are hoping for gourmet hot dogs.

However, the mountain can sleep tonight. We finally have the answer. The 2020 Ranger Round-Up Cook-Off will feature...

Mac 'n' Cheese.

That's right. To many folks, America's favorite take on a classic Italian dish is little more than a side. An afterthought. A starch!

They are wrong.

Mac 'n' Cheese is, in fact, a staple of good, old-fashioned comfort food. I know I speak for the town when I say I can't wait to find out what those rugged rangers can cook up.

For details on venue, date, and time, please contact event coordinator Margaret-June Flanagan.

Bo Delaney is an investigative reporter for the *Mountain Times*, covering local and late-breaking news around the mountain and in Maplewood.

MARGARET-JUNE WAS A character. That much was clear. Bo even considered featuring her for the Ranger Round-up expose. But once she began on a line of personal questioning, Margaret-June picked right up and shooed Bo away.

At one point in their phone call, Bo worked up the courage to hint at her relationship with Keegan. But, much to Bo's delight, Margaret-June already knew about it.

"I wasn't too sure about Keegan dating a Delaney girl," she had said. *"And least of all the black sheep."*

Bo had taken it as a compliment. She'd always identified that way—the outsider of her family. No husband. No children. No direction. But that reputation was slowly and surely changing, and even Margaret-June seemed to realize it, congratulating Bo on her recent articles and recognizing her for being the one to find the missing woman a couple weeks earlier. *"Keegan told me,"* she confessed. *"If only someone else reported that story—you'd get the glory* you're *due, young lady."*

That's where they disagreed. Bo did not want the spotlight for heroism. She didn't even want to be a hero. She wanted to write about them. Strictly. Which was why Bo was thrilled to learn the secret Margaret-June teased her with.

This year's Ranger Round-up was about more than a delectable pasta dish. And, Keegan's aunt added before Bo thanked her and hung up, even if Keegan didn't win the Mac 'n' Cheese Blue Ribbon, there might be a sweet consolation prize.

Chapter 20

Margaret called Keegan just as soon as Bo had the information she needed. "She's a lovely girl, Keegan. Really, she is."

"I agree. That's why I'm with her."

"And why is she with *you*?" Margaret pressed.

Keegan chuckled. "Good question, Aunt Marg."

"I'm only kidding. You're a catch, too. And you both love your jobs. She is a brave girl, Keegan. Don't let this one get away. All right?"

"I'm trying, Aunt Marg. Doing everything I can."

"And what's that? I didn't hear the clink of a heavy diamond on her finger over the phone."

Keegan groaned inwardly. "I don't know. I need to see if things fall into place at work. I want to offer Bo the world. Right now, all I can offer is a one-room cabin and more of the same."

Margaret let out a sigh on the other end of the phone. "Bo is not your mother, Keegan."

He scratched his chin and frowned. Keegan could always count on his father's sister to offer an... objective view of her sister-in-law.

"Here we go," he answered, standing from his office desk to get ready to head home for the day.

"No, no. I love Victoria. I do, Keegan. She's a good person. Different from us mountain people, but one of us, too. My point is that Bo isn't your mom. She loves her job, sure, but not because she wants to make a ton of money or live in the fanciest cabin on the mountain. And she likes her independence—I can see that. But she comes from that huge family. Five brothers and sisters, right? And she's here—where most of them live. It's fair to say that family is her priority. Whatever your reservations are, I will warn you, son: don't let them get in the way of a beautiful life."

Pushing a hand through his hair, he sucked in a breath. "Yeah. Yeah, I think you're right. Aunt Marg, I have to go. I have an errand to run before I get home tonight. And..." He checked his wristwatch. "I might not make it on time if I don't hurry."

Chapter 21

Something about what Margaret-June had said didn't sit right with Bo, and she got ready for the Ranger's Roundup under a general sense of unease.

Mary would go, which quelled Bo's nervousness a little, and Bo even asked her if she'd help Bo get ready after they checked in that morning's batch of guests.

"I've never once in my life helped you get dolled up. This is weird," Mary argued as they stood in Bo's room opposite the rustic vanity. Bo had laid out every single beautification product she owned—from eyelash curlers to a round brush to setting spray.

Bo shrugged. "I get the feeling that I need to look nice. People there know I'm writing a piece on it. And Keegan's competing with *our* recipe, so..."

"Don't you think you should be yourself, though?" Mary pointed out, pulling Bo's dark hair back and combing her fingers down through the long tresses.

Bo stared into her reflection, then glanced up at Mary. "Yeah. I do. But I also want to be a polished version of that. So we can skip the eyelash curlers, but I will stick with the black eyeliner. And it won't hurt to blow dry and hairspray my hair. You know, just for a little *pop*."

Mary grinned back at Bo and got to work, adding a little extra fluff here and smoothing there.

KEEGAN TOLD BO THAT he'd pick her up at a quarter to twelve. Event participants were to arrive at noon on the nose to submit their recipes and set up their dishes in warming trays.

This was the first year that the cook-off involved an oven dish—Margaret-June wasn't too happy about it, but she gave in when the votes were nearly unanimous in favor of mac 'n' cheese.

When they arrived at the BARn, Bo's brothers—the owners of the outdoor venue—gave their sister a hug and shook Keegan's hand. He pulled Alan aside and asked if Bo's dad was around. He said he had a question before things got rolling, though Bo couldn't imagine what he had to ask. Keegan knew her father, but only somewhat.

Alan ushered Keegan over to the original Delaney homestead, where the men shot the breeze for a while before Keegan returned to Bo's side in time to join her conversation with Margaret-June, who launched into a story about Keegan when he was a teenager.

It began awkwardly, and Bo wondered if the woman was fixing to undermine an otherwise lovely day.

"He talked about this girl in his Spanish class all of his senior year. I was just impressed there was a sophomore in an advanced Spanish class, but that's beside the point, I suppose," she rambled along. Bo finished setting out the paper plates and forks she'd brought for Keegan, taking care to fan out the napkins just so.

She glanced up to see Keegan grinning from ear to ear at his wacky aunt's reverie, and Bo tuned in.

"Anyway, he kept talking and talking about this girl before we realized it was Billy's little girlfriend. No one cared that Billy was dating her other than we felt bad for the poor thing. Billy was never as sweet-natured as his older brother."

Bo's eyes flashed up at Margaret-June then over to Keegan. She felt her cheeks grow red with embarrassment, but the older woman grabbed her wrist. "Bo, it was you. Keegan was always in love with you. Even in high school when you were dating his very own brother!"

Keegan moaned and shushed her. "Aunt Marg, you're embarrassing everyone, come on. Aren't you supposed to be helping the judges get ready?"

Margaret-June winked at Bo. "He better treat you well, Bo. You come tell me if he doesn't."

Bo smiled back and assured her that Keegan was as gentlemanly as could be.

Keegan gave her a squeeze around the waist then stood back from their position under a single tent. Bo joined him to assess the event.

Half a dozen other rangers had set up—their sous chefs assisting just like Bo. Alan and Robbie had the outdoor bar open and were serving beverages and burgers, just in case anyone wanted to pair a protein with their starch.

A local band had set up on the far field and was about to launch into their first set just as spectators, for lack of a better word, had trickled in.

"I'm not sure if I should hang here or wander around and take notes," Bo whispered up to Keegan.

He laced his fingers through hers and smiled down. "It's up to you. I'm okay here, if you need to interview anyone." He glanced around and bit down on his lower lip, chewing at it anxiously. "Hey, by the way, who are you interviewing for this feature?"

Bo lifted her eyebrows. "Good question. Your aunt asked that I wait until it was over, that way I could cover the winner—whoever it is."

"Well, what if it's me?" Keegan's mouth curled up in a mischievous smile.

Bo returned it and patted his arm. "Then I guess I have exclusive, early access to the hottest news in town, huh?"

Keegan didn't smile back. Instead, his face fell, turning unreadable. Bo frowned, confused. "What's wrong?"

He looked past her, and she turned to see Margaret-June advancing with a trio who could only be the amateur cook-off judges. Bo should know. She should have way more information on this event. Suddenly, she felt unprepared. Her stomach turned, and she began to feel as nervous as Keegan looked.

"Nothing," Keegan answered, squeezing her hand in his. "It's this stupid cook-off. I just—" he flashed his eyes again at the oncoming group and then looked at Bo.

"Hey, if it's the mac you're worried about, don't. That recipe is Mama Delaney crafted and approved. You're a shoo-in." Bo tried for a smile, but the air had shifted around them. A seriousness seemed to take effect, wrapping them together.

Keegan faced her and grabbed her other hand. "Bo, I have to talk to you."

Her breath hitched in her chest. "What?" she asked, her color draining as she looked up into Keegan's eyes.

"I can't wait any longer, I have to talk to you," he hissed, his eyes again darting past her.

Impending doom pushed the air out of Bo and she twisted to follow his gaze. Still just Margaret-June and three vaguely familiar faces. "Keegan, you're scaring me. What?"

Without an answer, he tugged her hand away from their tent and the four steaming trays of Mama's Mountain Mac.

He half dragged, half ushered her through the other half of the competitors' tents and back behind the outdoor bar until they were hidden among twisted alligator junipers and a thick grove of oak trees.

Bo felt Keegan's hand tremble in hers as he finally stopped and turned to face her, looking down into her eyes as he lowered himself to the forest floor.

She frowned, bewildered, until—he pulled a small velvet box from his jacket pocket with his free hand.

"Roberta—I mean Bo—" he stuttered, fumbling single handedly with the box until he released her hand and held the precious container in both of his. With one knee firmly planted in the earth, he opened the box and revealed a stunning white gold ring with a princess-cut diamond protruding from its satin bed. "Bo, will you marry me?"

She fell into his arms, unable to speak for some moments. He hugged her with one arm, the other careful to keep the box safe from Bo's shock. Pushing back, she examined the jewel and then searched Keegan's eyes. "Are you serious? Is this your... your mom's?"

He nodded. "I'm sorry for being a little... slow to come around, I guess. Bo, I want to give you everything. I don't have all that yet, but I can give you this and it comes with my mom's blessing. I don't know what you said to her, but she asked me to visit two nights ago. She said she wanted to talk to me and give me something. Or, give *us* something." Again he lifted the box.

She studied it, the light catching in Bo's bright eyes until they danced back to him. "It's perfect. You're perfect, Keegan. This—" she waved her hand around them, indicating the vast forest and private hamlet they'd stumbled into, "is perfect."

"You never answered my question," he prompted, drawing his hand to her face and lifting her chin.

Bo's cheeks flushed, and she rushed to answer. "Yes. Yes, I'll marry you. I love you, Keegan."

He pressed his lips against her while blindly finding her left ring finger and sliding the ring over her knuckle and into position.

Bo kissed him back and the million worries that had been rolling around in his head suddenly came to a stop. Keegan had not quite realized that, because everything was amazing before this moment—now everything would be perfect. Promotion or no promotion. Wherever Bo wanted to work or write. This commitment meant more to him than anything else. He never realized it could.

All Bo needed was a promise. And all Keegan needed was to have Bo as his Maplewood Mountain bride.

Chapter 22

THE RANGER WHO HAS IT ALL

By Bo Delaney, *Mountain Times*

MAPLEWOOD—Droves of locals and tourists alike flocked to Maplewood's Annual Ranger Round-up this past Saturday, held at the BARn. Event attendees had the pleasure of enjoying not just the varieties of macaroni and cheese on display, but also a local music group, craft beer, home-grilled burgers, and even Leslie Zick's assortment of apple pies a la mode as a sweet surprise to culminate the winner's ceremony.

Though readers might enjoy learning about the atmosphere of the event, most only care about one thing: who won?

By the end of the ceremony, event coordinator Margaret-June Flanagan named the best three macaroni makers on the mountain.

In third place, with a southwest take on the dish, came Ranger Brian Gruber. Gruber's mac 'n' cheese arrested the senses with hints of jalapeno and an aftertaste of subtle cayenne pepper.

Title of runner-up went to retired Sheriff Doug Elkton. Elkton, together with his wife, Betty, offered a smooth-as-velvet concoction for the judges and event-goers. His creamy dish was favored by some but still couldn't pull off the win.

Which brings us to the 2020 Rangers Round-up Mac 'n' Cheese Cook-off Winner. First place in this year's event officially went to none other than Ranger Keegan Flanagan.

Flanagan, with only a pinch of help from his fiancée—that's right, this ranger is taken, ladies—scored bonus points for sticking to a classic, down-home rendition of America's favorite side. Affectionately called "Mama's Mountain Mac," Flanagan's golden-crusted dish was enjoyed by tasters young and old, of simple palettes and refined, making him a winner across all categories.

But that wasn't the only win for Ranger Flanagan on Saturday. No, no. In fact, surprising all the attendees was Flanagan's chief, who announced publicly that Keegan had earned a long-sought-after promotion within the department.

Though Flanagan had not made his aspirations previously known, he'd been working hard to secure the

THE RANGER'S MOUNTAIN BRIDE

title of Search and Rescue Coordinator for Apache County. This promotion comes with new responsibilities; however, Ranger Flanagan remains humble. "It's my duty to serve the mountain. I'm excited to be selected for the position, but my priority is and always will be my family. Speaking of which," Flanagan goes on to joke toward the end of the interview, "I'd better get going. I believe my fiancée needs my help to plan a wedding."

For details on the Flanagan-Delaney wedding venue, date, and time, please contact wedding planners Margaret-June Flanagan and Mary Delaney.

Bo Delaney is a human interest writer for the *Mountain Times* and now engaged to be married.

Epilogue

Six Months Later

Mountain Weddings

DELANEY & FLANAGAN

Roberta "Bo" Delaney and Keegan Robert Flanagan were married in a Catholic Ceremony at St. Ann's of the Holy Trinity, Maplewood, at 5:00pm, Saturday, the 3rd of October 2020. The wedding was blessed by Father Christopher Michaels and followed by a reception at the Wood Smoke Lodge.

The bride wore ivory and lace, which beautifully contrasted with the black, cocktail length dresses of her bridal party. The groom made for a dashing sight in a black suit, cowboy hat, and boots. The bouquet and floral arrangements were filled with locally sourced foliage, solidifying Bo and the wedding as the epitome of mountain chic.

The reception was as lovely and meaningful as the ceremony, tucked cozily into the fir trees and maples that spread from an expansive back deck off into the

THE RANGER'S MOUNTAIN BRIDE 109

national forest. A full dance floor rocked the bed of the mountain as wedding guests line-danced and two-stepped the night away.

Spanning from 6:00pm into the early morning hours of Sunday, the reception ended with party-worn guests content to have celebrated one of Maplewood's happiest couples, leaving the bride and groom to begin their honeymoon with their first night as man and wife in Wood Smoke Lodge.

Bo and Keegan will continue their honeymoon with a week on the beaches of Mexico, where they plan to relax and soak up the sun before returning to the mountain to serve their community.

Some may say it was love at first sight for the couple... back at Maplewood High, where they shared some classes but never connected. It wasn't until the bride's return to the mountain that a romance could flourish. A chance meeting in Big Ed's Country Market developed into a warm courtship and soon evolved into a deep and lasting love.

The couple plans to live in Keegan's Maplewood cabin while they work on expanding it to fit what will hopefully one day be a big, happy, mountain family.

From all of us at the Mountain Times to the newlyweds, cheers to many happy and fruitful years.

Did you enjoy this story? Order *The Cowboy's Mountain Bride* today.

A Note from the Author

Thank you for reading this copy of *The Ranger's Mountain Bride*. If you have a moment, I'd be very grateful if you'd considering leaving your review on Amazon[1], BookBub[2], and Goodreads[3].

Let's stay in touch!

You can find me on Facebook, Instagram, Twitter, Pinterest, and through my website at elizabethbromke.com[4]. I love to hear from readers. Add me on social media, join my newsletter, or send me an email. I'd love to connect.

Truly,
Elizabeth

---

1. https://www.amazon.com/dp/B07WCQLTMK
2. https://www.bookbub.com/books/the-ranger-s-mountain-bride-married-in-maplewood-maplewood-book-5-by-elizabeth-bromke
3. https://www.goodreads.com/book/show/47838183-the-ranger-s-mountain-bride?from_search=true
4. https://www.elizabethbromke.com/

About the Author

Elizabeth Bromke is the author of the Maplewood Sisters saga and the Hickory Grove series. She loves writing sweet romance, women's fiction, and suspense.

Elizabeth lives in a small mountain town in Arizona. There, she enjoys her own happily-ever-after with her husband and their young son.

Read more at https://www.elizabethbromke.com/.

Made in the USA
Middletown, DE
05 January 2021